# MIKO KINGS

An Indian Baseball Story

LeAnne Howe

*Aunt Lute Books, San Francisco*

All historical photographs (including cover photos) appear courtesy of *The Ada Evening News*.

Chapter 6 appears, in slightly different form, in *The Yalobusha Review*, vol. XII, 2007, Univ. of Mississippi, Oxford.

The author would like to acknowledge the song "The Ball Is Over," originally published in a Greeley newspaper (date unknown), and re-published in Charles Saulsberry's 1940 *Daily Oklahoman* series "Fifty Years of Baseball." The song that appears here, *"After the bases are gone...,"* is the author's homage to "The Ball Is Over."

Lyrics to the Beatles song "Because" reprinted with permission from Sony/ATV Music Publishing LLC.

Aunt Lute Books
P.O. Box 410687
San Francisco, CA 94141
www.auntlute.com

Executive Director: Joan Pinkvoss
Artistic Director: Shay Brawn

Production: Erica Bestpitch, Andrea de Brito, KB Burnside, Gina Gemello, Shahara Godfrey, Cloé-Mai Le Gall-Scoville, Cassie McGettigan, Soma Nath, Anna Neary, Sabrina Peterson, Kathleen Pullum, Elisabeth Rohrbach, Jenna Varden, Melissa Wong-Shing, Ladi Youssefi.

Cover and Text Design: Amy Woloszyn | amymade graphic design

This book was funded in part by grants from the LEF Foundation, the National Endowment for the Arts, and the Vessel Foundation.

**Library of Congress Cataloging-in-Publication Data**
Howe, LeAnne.
    Miko Kings : an Indian baseball story / LeAnne Howe. -- 1st ed.
        p. cm.
    ISBN 978-1-879960-78-7 (alk. paper)
    1. Indian baseball players--Fiction. 2. Choctaw Indians--Fiction. 3. Ada (Okla.)--Fiction. 4. Baseball stories. I. Title.

PS3608.O95M56 2006
813'.6--dc22

                                                                    2007006850

Printed in the U.S.A. on acid-free paper
First Edition 10 9 8 7 6 5 4

# Acknowledgments

There are many people to thank for their generous support in bringing *Miko Kings* to life. Barry Hannah, for bringing me to the University of Mississippi as the 2006-2007 John and Renee Grisham Writer-in-Residence. The fellowship gave me the time to finish the book. Sincere thanks also goes to Professors Michelle Raheja, University of California, Riverside; Reed Browning, Kenyon College; Susan Strauss, Michigan State University; Philip Deloria, University of Michigan, for introducing me to *His Last Game;* Roy Wortman, Kenyon College; Annette Trefzer, University of Mississippi, and her husband Mickey Howley; Robert Warrior, University of Oklahoma, for passing along research from Carlisle Indian Industrial School; Jacki Rand, University of Iowa, for her careful reading; Lauri Sisquoc, Museum Curator, Sherman Indian School (Riverside, California); poet Susan Swartout for her encouragement all these years; Ron Pinkard, for our many intellectual discussions about *Okchamali;* and Amelia A. Rogers at the University of Mississippi, for her patience and help in creating the images. A special thanks to Alberta Blackburn, Billie Floyd, Brenda Tollett, Daisy Daggs, and Zelda Daggs for their expertise and knowledge on the history of Ada, Oklahoma. Thanks also to filmmaker Jim Fortier for helping me believe in images, and to Susan Power, who strongly urged me to follow the characters wherever they took me. *Yakoke* to all the Indian ballplayers and ball teams that play every August at the Choctaw Nation's Red Warrior's Park in Tuskahoma, Oklahoma.

Special thanks to Joan Pinkvoss for not giving up on me, or the novel. Gina Gemello, ditto, and to all the women at Aunt Lute Books. Many thanks to Deia de Brito for creating Ezol on the page, as well as to author and baseball historian Royce "Crash" Parr and his wife Sheila for their generous help with Oklahoma baseball history research.

And finally a very special thanks to my son Joseph Craig and his partner Sharon Moseley, who helped me create the baseball scenes in this story.

*For all the American Indians who've played the game!*

# MIKO
# KINGS

And here too is the echo of baseball's childhood memory in *Anompa Sipokni,* Old Talking Places. Indian Territory.

*A book.*

*The film.*

*His Last Game*. Released in 1909 by International Moving Pictures.

*The Story.*

# Prelude

A peach moon slowly rises at the hem of the sky. Here, September sunlight turns grainy at twilight, as the brilliant azure of the midday sky fades to robin's-egg blue. In a half hour, balmy air will descend, signaling to the locust choir nestled on the limbs of a nearby oak tree that it's time to travel again. Hunt a mate. Compete for love.

Meanwhile...

A few yards away at Eldo Whipple's Chicken Farm outside of Ada, fourteen Indians dressed in a variety of stage costumes await another kind of signal. A cue from their moving picture producer Carl Laemmle. Four of the men wear short-sleeve shirts that say "Jimtown Bar." The others have flimsy strips of cloth pinned on the front of their baseball shirts that read "Choctaw."

Their long hair shorn and their faces scrubbed clean, the Choctaws wear clothes cut from modern textiles, the same as any Broadway clerk. They represent savagery gone civilized. Laemmle tells the Choctaws to "act jolly," as if they were enjoying wearing long johns, socks, and tight shoes.

In real life the Indians are professional baseball players for the Miko Kings, winners of the 1907 Indian Territory League pennant. But today they're acting in the first moving picture about American baseball. The story, set in Indian Territory, is about two rival teams, the fictional Jimtown Bar team and the Choctaw Indians. Everyone associated with the Miko Kings has been drafted to play a role in the film, which is called *His Last Game*.

The Miko Kings' best hurler, twenty-five year old Hope Little Leader, has had a remarkable year, finishing the season with an earned run average of 2.17. Today, he's made up to look like an aging, stoic plains warrior. He wears a black wig with two long braids, black shirt, a tan vest with blue horses painted on it, leggings, and moccasins. The wig's supposed to make him look traditional, but Laemmle wove it like a girl's braids. It's obvious to the Indians that their producer doesn't know the difference between the plaits of a powerful warrior and those of a little girl. Each time Laemmle's back is turned, Hope's teammates elbow one another and point at the wig. The men use sign language to call Hope *Ohoyo Holba,* like a woman but not.

Hope watches his teammates joke at his expense. He signs back that he's the hero of this story: "Out of 157 games played this season, I've started in 45, completed 40, won 35, and lost 8." He signs the number 8 again for emphasis.

The men snicker. Hope signals Blip Bleen, the Miko Kings' player-manager. "Tell them I'm the hero," he signs.

Blip takes one look at Hope and yells toward the other men, "Dang, if you ain't the ugliest Indian gal I've ever seen!"

A Chickasaw-Choctaw, Blip is also the batting champion for the Miko Kings. He's hit .334 this season, earning him a fourth batting crown in the I.T. League. Today Blip dons a feathered headdress, leather-fringed war shirt, and leggings. His character represents another throwback to progress.

Hope walks over to Blip, who's standing next to the "Jimtown Bar," which in reality is the chicken coop on Whipple's Farm.

"I'm supposed to restore the team's confidence in the old ways," Hope says. He pulls a piece of paper out of his back pocket and begins reading aloud. "It says right here: 'Bill Going is the pitcher's name. He's the hero of the story and embodies the feral native in his natural habitat—undomesticated, untamed, and uncorrupted.'"

Blip grins. "You bet." He strikes a match and lights the peace pipe that Laemmle has given him as a prop. "For an undomesticated feller, you read pretty good." Blip slowly exhales smoke into the air. "Don't worry," he says, "in a hundred years no one will even remember our names."

Hope kicks the dirt and walks away. He looks ridiculous, he just knows it. In fact, they all look preposterous. But no matter how much he protests, Laemmle just shakes his head and says, "A perfect foil. A perfect foil." Hope has no idea what a "foil" is, but he wishes he'd never agreed to play it.

Making a moving picture is a new experience for the team. After finishing a 24-game winning streak that clinched the Indian Territory League pennant, the Miko Kings boarded the train to Chicago to play in a series of pick-up games. They had one awful outing against Chicago's Doc White, one of the American League's best pitchers. But Hope found his arm in the bottom of the third and, with his own 1-2-3 chucks, dispensed Chicago's three best hitters in twelve pitches, and Miko Kings finished second in the series.

Henri Day, Miko Kings' owner, was shocked when the *Chicago Tribune* published a semi-fictitious story about the team that pitted "the red man against the white man." The August 10, 1907 headline read, "Custer's Last Stand, Strike Two." At first Henri took offense because the reporter didn't know the difference between the Choctaws, one of the Five Civilized Tribes from Indian Territory, and the Sioux of the Northern Plains.

"For Christ's sake!" said Henri. "The Sioux do not have a professional baseball team. Not now, and at the rate white folks are trying to kill them, maybe never."

But when Carl Laemmle arrived at their hotel the next morning, Henri (himself a Choctaw) learned the public relations value of being labeled a wild Sioux Indian. Laemmle said he owned a string of nickelodeons in Chicago and that he wanted to make a moving picture about real Indians.

"People want to see moving pictures that are realistic," said Laemmle. "There's heaps of money to be made from pictures about the noble red man." The two men shook hands and agreed that if the Miko Kings appeared in the film, Laemmle would correctly identify the team as Choctaw.


Back on the moving picture set... Laemmle's photographer barks orders at Hope from across Eldo Whipple's chicken yard.

"Hey, *yoose dere!* In the black wig. Understand English?"

Hope nods to show that he does.

"Do not gaze directly into Lumiére!" The photographer points at his camera and repeats his warning again. Slowly.

Hope shouts, "Okay!" He straightens the wig on his head and watches as a young boy shoos an angry bantam rooster off the makeshift diamond. Until today the young immigrant was unloading railroad cars at the Frisco Depot. The boy speaks very little English. Everyone remarks on how lucky it is that Laemmle and the boy both speak Jewish.

A short distance away, Laemmle arranges the six extras dressed in black hats and black coats at the gravesite. What a bunch of cutups, thinks Hope. Three weeks ago, no one could have imagined that they'd all be in pictures. Even Henri's oddball niece Ezol is playing a role, a male gravedigger. Laemmle told Ezol she had to keep the black hat pulled low to hide the fact that she's a woman. Now her biggest challenge is being able to see to dig the grave.

Hope stands in the yard with his arms crossed, waiting with a kind of aloof detachment. He watches his teammates some fifty yards away clown and lark about. Occasionally their laughter rises on the wind and a word or two drifts in his direction. "Savage curveball" and "batting on third" are old stories, but "a one cut woman" is new. It vaguely interests him—until he feels something strike his big toe. He looks down and sighs. A little red hen is pecking his moccasins. He tenderly picks her up. "You don't like being boxed in on allotment land, do you?" He holds her out in front of him and she clucks nervously, flapping out of his grasp. "Me neither," he says, as chicken feet and feathers tumble downward.

A strong gust whips bits of sand in his face and he notices an eerie, bluish-green cloud moving up from the south. Now even the chickens run for cover. Suddenly Hope is afraid. It's true he wants to become famous as a great baseball pitcher, but not as some chucklehead in the nickelodeons. He decides to quit. Head for home. It's bad luck playing make-believe. He strides to the gate and unties his mare. He grabs the reins and effortlessly jumps in the saddle just as Laemmle calls his name.

"Mr. Little Leader, we're ready. Please take your place on the ballfield—without your baseball glove."

Hope hesitates, weighing the situation, as Laemmle walks over to him. He dismounts and the two men confer out of earshot of the others. No one knows exactly what is said, but eventually Hope ties his horse back at the gate and joins the others. The producer flashes the signal. The camera begins rolling and Hope Little Leader winds up for the first pitch, caught between his dreams of grandeur and the dark stream on the horizon that awaits them all.

# 1

## Restoration

### Ada, Oklahoma, Summer 2006

As I stand in the middle of the living room in my house on Ninth Street, a carpenter swings a sledgehammer like a baseball bat into the lath and plaster wall.

*Whack.*

The lath caves in and bits of plaster fly across the room. He then leans the sledgehammer against a metal trash can and uses a claw hammer to jerk the small strips of wood outward. Weathered plaster, the color of dirty limestone, falls onto the floor. His helper comes into the room, picks up the sledgehammer, and begins to pound the wall again.

*Whack. Whack. Whack.*

In moments the room is filled with a chalky plaster dust. I walk outside and shake my protective mask. Even ten feet away I can hear chunks of plaster hitting the floor like rocks.

*Whack.*

Something about that sound...I close my eyes and am hurled back in time. Eight months ago: November 9, 2005. Amman, Jordan. I'm running toward the sound of breaking glass. The ground shakes and I fall to my knees and cover my face. Flying glass cuts both arms, but I won't notice the bloodstain on my white jacket until much later. Another explosion. I freeze. A large metal door rockets to the ground. I jump up and sprint toward the Days Inn. *My friend's in there...*

"Lena?"

"Yes?" I open my eyes.

The carpenter is beside me, looking at me quizzically. "You okay?" I nod. "Come take a look at this," he says. I put my mask on and follow him inside. He points to the breach he's made, then reaches down and pulls out a dusty U.S. mail pouch that's been hidden inside the wall. He knocks years of fine dust off the brown leather and hands it to me.

"This isn't something you see every day," he says. "Know how it got here?"

"No, I'm just as surprised as you."

"See if there's stolen money inside. Wouldn't that be something!"

It takes a bit of doing, but finally I'm able to unfasten the brass buckle on the pouch. I leaf through the contents. "Shoot," I say. "Nothing but papers." We joke about the famous bank robbers that came through Ada, then I put the pouch in the back bedroom and resume my work, sanding layers of colors off the kitchen cabinets. First blue, then green, and finally a colorless beige shows through as I push the electric sander against the doors. I force myself to ignore the sounds of the sledgehammer.

The land and the house once belonged to my Choctaw grandmother, MourningTree Bolin. I inherited it when she died nineteen years ago, and it has remained vacant until now. Although the roof is nearly caving in, it has solid oak flooring, a deep front porch with red brick pylons, and lovely wide eaves. When I first entered the front room after being away for so long, the majestic fireplace that once heated the house immediately captured my imagination. I could almost smell a fire blazing in the hearth, feel the heat of the crackling blackjack logs, hear the muffled voices of Indians gathered in the room. The image was so pleasing that my first remodeling decision was to have the ugly gas heater insert removed. It had been stuck in the hearth since the year I was born.

Later that evening, after the workmen leave, I gently wipe the pouch's brown leather with a wet sponge and rub it with Lexol to soften it. At one time a leather shoulder strap must have been attached to each side, but it's missing. The pouch is stuffed with papers, some in a childish hand, others typed, some penned by an adult. There are handwritten pages of symbols and numbers, letters, newspaper clippings, and a 12 x 12 black and white photograph of an Indian baseball team. There is also a decaying journal with the name "Ezol" embossed on the cover. The spine is broken, its pages loose and catty-cornered every which way. It appears to me as if someone had hastily torn through the journal and ripped out pages, then retied the contents with a satin ribbon to hold it together. I don't untie the ribbon for fear the pages will crumble in my hands.

The photograph has "1907 Miko Kings Champions" scrawled across the bottom. At the sight of the picture, I draw in a breath of satisfaction, a feeling so rare that I am taken aback. What a thrill to have known such men. Though thinking about who they were and what they were like is probably more satisfying than the reality, I know. When I was a child, my father was heroic to me only because I rarely saw him. He was a truck driver, a Sac and Fox from Stroud. I was often left for weeks at a time with friends or a maiden aunt of his. I can remember looking at his picture and counting the days until his return. But when he finally came home to pick up the dog and me, he was exhausted. All he did was sleep until he'd leave again.

Soon after the discovery, the contents of the leather pouch began to haunt me. I decided to ask my neighbor, Mr. Ellis, an elderly man in his eighties, if he'd ever heard of the Miko Kings. He said he hadn't, but that in the early years of Ada—during his grandfather's time—there were Indian baseball teams galore and that I should look through the local newspaper archives. Good advice, but it would have to wait. I was occupied with the ongoing construction. If I was going to make my living as a freelance journalist in the middle of Oklahoma, I needed a place where I could live and work.

But a couple of weeks later, I still couldn't stop thinking about the mail pouch, especially the photo. Photography has always had the ability to record the visible world with a kind of notional truth. The faces of the Indian men in the picture are compelling, even handsome. Their expressions give no hint of the context of their lives. For instance, nothing in the image reveals the frustration, the anger they must have felt—they were living through the worst part of the Allotment Era. Initiated by the Dawes Act of 1887, the Allotment Era lasted for forty-seven years. During that time, the federal government privatized all of the tribal lands of Indian Territory into individual plots, much of it going to non-Indians. What I know about allotment is burned into me from my grandmother's tirades. "Think of it, Lena!" she would hiss. "An entire race of people is swindled out of their land by changing the pronouns? Ours to mine. We to I. Words are power. They change everything."

Yet when I look at the photograph, I'm unable to read anger. Instead, I note the stormy clouds in the background that must have been moving across the prairie when the picture was taken. There is also a touch of naiveté in the nine dark Indians dressed in matching ball caps and uniforms. They look steadily into the camera's eye. Their heads tilt forward ever so slightly as they lean on bats and clutch baseballs. Although the image is nearly a hundred years old, it isn't an Edward Curtis-style photograph, with the Indians portrayed as either noble savages or stoic warriors. The men in my photo seem neither humble nor bloated with self-confidence.

Three of the Indians that stand in the back row wear suit coats and bowler hats. They don't appear to be part of the team—who are they? Perhaps owners or investors, or maybe umpires. One of the players has a deep scar that runs from the top of his right eyebrow onto his cheekbone. His left hand is cupped around the knob of the bat. He's locked in silence along with all the others, yet his eyes seemed to be looking directly at me. While I'd never had any interest in baseball, the player with the scar on his face captured my imagination. Who was he? And who did the pouch belong to? My grandmother? If not, who could have hidden it inside the wall of her house?

My grandmother had told me she'd built the house on her family's allotment land in 1906, when she was only seventeen. This was a full year before statehood. Now when friends and neighbors come by, they remark on the bold sophistication that permeates the small Craftsman home. I'd always assumed that she'd used up all her elegance when she built the house—its understatement and design seemed so unlike her, the woman I often found sitting on the back porch in a bright pink dress, smoking one cigarette after another.

When MourningTree passed away in 1987, she was ninety-eight. She'd outlived her husband, Hank Bolin—and, much to her eternal sorrow, my mother, Kit Bolin Coulter, who died giving birth to me.

When I was a little girl, Grandmother did her best to gift me memories of my mother. She presented me with a satin-covered shoebox of keepsakes with "Lena Coulter" embroidered on the top. In it were Mother's baby shoes. Her Gibson guitar picks. A lock of dark brown hair, a few pictures, a 1904 Indian-head penny, and sundry other items. In the pictures Mother looks tall and thin. Gorgeous even. For a time she'd been a successful country-western singer with a big alto voice, I'd been told. But Kit Bolin Coulter died of uremic poisoning a week after I was born. In 1959, there wasn't much the doctors could do for the fifty-one-year-old Choctaw woman who was having her first baby. I've never been able to visualize my mother from the stories about her. I'd always pretend for Grandmother's sake that I could find her in my box of memories. But she wasn't there. I felt she'd abandoned me—that somehow my umbilical cord to the center of her had been severed, completely detached before I was born, setting me adrift to fend for myself, with only an absent father.

I spent every summer with my grandmother in Ada, at her insistence. She would teach me Choctaw words, and how to pronounce them properly. I don't think I retained all that much because we'd begin every lesson with the same words and expressions. She showed me how to pound corn with a pestle and fan the husks, the same way Choctaws have processed *tanchi* for a thousand years. We'd often make *banaha,* bean bread, and the Choctaw specialty, *pashofa,* a corn soup flavored with oak ash.

On Saturdays, we'd bake "washday cobbler," a cross between pie and bread, made with blackberries, huckleberries, or peaches. At least once a week, we'd go fishing for sun perch at a small pond in nearby

Byng. Often on these excursions she would dip her hands in pond water and pat me down from head to toe, all the while singing the "cool off song," not a tuneful melody, but more of a chant. Grandmother said her song was to prevent a fire from growing in my belly. Sometimes she'd weep and say, "My girl, my girl. It's not your fault. It's not your fault. The fault is all mine."

I didn't need an explanation for why she cried. I knew it was because she resented me for being born. She just couldn't get over the fact that I'd grown in her daughter's body, and the shell of her gave way in order that I might live—nothing could change that between the two of us.


When I moved to New York in 1982, I believed I would never return to Oklahoma. At twenty-three, I wanted to forget that I was half Choctaw and half Sac and Fox. Forget all things Okie, like twangy country-western music. Pitchers of 3.2 beer. The po-lice. The way I looked—long black hair, brown eyes, and a sturdy build—I knew I could pass for Italian, Mexican, or French, especially in New York.

I landed a low-wage job with Condé Nast Publications. Although I was a glorified gofer, I learned enough to be hired as a real editorial assistant for *Vanity Fair* in 1983. As a beginning writer I was assigned to research, and had to contribute three short news stories per week to the various magazines owned by the corporation. Over the next nine years, I moved up through the publishing ranks and began writing short features for *Condé Nast Traveler*. But in 1994, I decided to quit. I was restless and wanted to see the world—a cliché, I knew, but it was true. I wanted to live out of the country. For a couple of years, I'd been off and on with a freelance photographer named Sayyed Farhan, a Palestinian who'd been making a successful living working abroad. Why not me? By then I had dozens of editorial contacts with magazines all over Europe. I'd read that after the first Gulf War, the Middle East was going to become the next travel frontier for Americans. King Hussein of Jordan had signed a historic peace treaty between his country and Israel, and American companies and NGOs were moving there in droves. I believed I could write and produce enough articles about traveling throughout the Middle East to support myself. So I relocated to Amman.

I began by writing about the sixth-century monastery of Saint Catherine in the Sinai Desert, the world's oldest Souk in Damascus, the city of Palmyra, and the Nabataean trading center Petra in southern Jordan, where Cleopatra once caravanned to meet her lover, Mark Antony. I wrote about my personal encounters with Syrians, Egyptians, and Bedouin, and what it was like to be a tourist in the Holy Lands. My work then led me to the virtual world of online publications, increasing my income considerably.

I learned to speak Arabic like a foreigner. From my base in Amman, I traveled extensively, made friends, and rekindled my relationship with Sayyed. I had in mind to write a series of travel books about the *new* Middle East: "Tour Amman on $20 a Day," that type of thing. The plan evaporated on September 11th with the bombing of the World Trade Center.

After the U.S. invasion of Iraq in 2003, I began to dress differently. I often wore all black and covered my hair with a white hijab. I tried to stand out in the crowd, though not as an American. I wanted to be mistaken for the American-educated daughter of a wealthy Jordanian, which would protect me somewhat from the Iraqi *shebab*—single men under thirty pouring into Amman since the invasion. I repeatedly said, *"Aboui Arabi."* My father's an Arab.

As my freelance work dwindled to nothing, I began working as an office temp for UNICEF and other NGOs. Then last November, in 2005, my life in Amman unraveled. As had been our custom when he came to town, I'd taken a taxi to meet Sayyed at the Days Inn. Often we'd spend afternoons in the lounge reading the *Guardian* or the *New York Times,* snacking on the *mubassal,* onion pancakes, and drinking *shai,* a sweet Arabic tea laced with fresh mint. But on that day, he'd been hired to take pictures of the hotel for their website. The taxi driver dropped me off a few blocks away so I could buy us a sweet. Then the explosions and, later, the news that the death roll was sixty people—including Sayyed.

During the next couple of months, I would sit on my apartment's balcony and—according to strict Islamic doctrine—sin. But because I am neither Muslim nor Christian, I drank gin and tonics morning, noon, and night. I brooded. Even my friends' pity annoyed me. I'd grown weary of being an expatriate, of always being called on to explain or defend America's actions. Besides, I had my own problems with America, especially its treatment of American Indians. I regularly questioned who I was—an Indian from Oklahoma, always *from,* but forever absent? Of course, I'd returned home for cursory visits. There was my father's funeral in Stroud in 1995, and a friend's wedding. But without meaning to I'd become a nomad, searching the world for something I couldn't quite name.

Then, in early April, I heard a strange voice at dusk during the *Salaat.* In Arab countries the *Salaat* is chanted five times a day, the last at sunset. That evening, a light breeze tickled the sands of the Arabian Desert, and through a veil of sunlight the whole of Amman seemed covered in a glittering fairy dust. But instead of *"Allahu Akbar"* I heard *"The time has come to return home."* The next morning at sunrise it was the same. *The time has come to return home.* Without warning, I began to sob. So I hadn't purged all my Native connections after all. Even though I'd put ten thousand miles between me and Oklahoma, the land of my ancestors had tracked me down and was speaking. At age forty-seven, I clung to it like a lamp against the darkness. I sold everything I had. Within a month I extricated myself from where I had thought I might be for the rest of my life.

A few weeks after the construction on the house was complete, I began in earnest to discover what had happened to the Miko Kings. On the back of the photograph was "September 1907" and a list of names. The handwriting was very small and the names of the players were block printed. Did my grandmother write this? Did she know the Indian baseball players? She must have. But why had she never mentioned them? Or even that she'd known Indians who were baseball players?

I didn't know anything about Indian baseball teams around Ada, but my experience as a journalist and researcher taught me that I should be able to find the answers. I started with a visit to the Oklahoma Historical Society's archives in Oklahoma City to see if any documents on Indian baseball teams existed. Nothing. Following up on Mr. Ellis' advice, I read hundreds of pages of old newspapers from local towns around Ada on microfiche, looking for stories about the individual players. Another dead end. I asked around Ada if anyone could remember where the old ballpark had been. Most folks didn't even know that Ada had a ballpark in 1907. However, a woman at the Ada Historical Society found some of the players listed in the 1900 census records of Pontotoc County. When that was all the information she was able to recover, she suggested I go back through the mail pouch to see if I could find any other clues.

When I removed all the documents again, I found a small piece of paper stuck to the bottom of the bag. At first I was afraid I'd tear it when pulling it loose. But I carefully picked it out—a yellow, stiffened newspaper clipping.

# THE ADA WEEKLY NEWS.
## July 10, 1904
### BASEBALL

Indian-owned ball club Miko Kings took the MKT train northwest for an exhibition game against the El Reno Sharpshooters in a lavish July 4 celebration, at which the Kiowas killed a jersey cow in mock-rodeo style, then barbecued and devoured the remains in front of the grandstand. MK's newest spitballer, Hope Little Leader, objected to the umpire, named John Coffee, citing this man's ancestor as having forced the Choctaws on the infamous "Trail of Tears." Little Leader refused to pitch and El Reno, in turn, refused to pay Miko Kings' bill at the Lightfoot Hotel.

There was considerable commotion on El Reno's side. Finally, the dispute was resolved and the sheriff was brought in to umpire the three-game series. He called the game with two six-shooters, one in each holster. The first two games went to El Reno, 14-5 and 11-2. Miko Kings had better hitting, and as owner Henri Day reported, perhaps "better" umpiring, as the sheriff was called away. The last game went to Miko Kings, 7-3.

Next week Miko Kings is set to play Tishomingo, followed by Wapanucka and Ardmore.

I returned in earnest to the microfiche and began reading through hundreds of pages of newspaper. Day after day I read reel after reel. Eventually I realized there weren't any personal accounts of the players because at the turn of the century there were no sportswriters in Indian Territory. There were reporters, but they were writing about shootings, stabbings, hangings, major fires, and obituaries. I did manage to find a couple of notices about the games, but no individual stories. No one was recording the players' family lives, or writing about the team's rivalries. Finally, disheartened, I gave up.

It was then that Ezol appeared. Perhaps my need to know brought her across time and space. Her spirit entered the house and placed the team's history on my shoulders, heavy as foreign epaulets.

That night, she unwrapped the team's stories as one might open birthday gifts. Out of order, but with a passion for celebration. Out came memories of glorious summer days and baseball diamonds blistered by blue skies and hot winds. Out came Ada's storefronts and boardwalks. Eye-catchers and newspapers. Fireflies and fastballs.

She sprinkled her baseball stories with words like "up-down," "inshoot," and other terms I was unfamiliar with. She also talked about a silent film entitled *His Last Game,* and its producer, Carl Laemmle. She said the film depicted a Choctaw baseball pitcher, set amidst a murder plot. Yet the biggest problem Laemmle had was keeping a banty rooster off the makeshift ballfield. She told me she had been an extra in the film.

When at last she finally placed her delicate hands over the black and white image, she murmured softly, "This is the only photograph that exists of the Miko Kings. It was taken at the Ada ballpark just before they played Fort Sill's Seventh Cavalrymen for the Twin Territories championship. The year is 1907. Here is what you see."


Catcher Albert Goingsnake snatches up a ground ball and shoots it to Isom Joel at second, who pivots and fires to Lucius Mummy on first. Everyone watching the team warm up knows they're about to witness the greatest Indian ball club ever assembled, because once the season ends, the future of the Twin Territories League is uncertain. On

November 16, 1907, in less than two months, Indian Territory is being legislated out of existence, along with Oklahoma Territory. A state is being sewn together from two parts. With the creation of Oklahoma, with the privatization of tribal lands, everything changes. Indians will be written out of Oklahoma's picture. And history.

But Hope Little Leader doesn't care about this. His only thoughts are about pitching a no-hitter against the Seventh Cavalrymen. Before going out to the mound to start batting practice, he pulls a pock-marked bat out of a potato sack and hands it to Blip Bleen, player-manager for the Miko Kings. Bleen, the most powerful hitter in the Indian Territory League, has already socked an incredible twenty-seven home runs during an eighty-nine game stretch. An unheard of number considering it's the era of the dead-ball.

Goingsnake holds his catcher's mitt, a homemade leather pancake permanently dented from years of abuse. He stands next to Blip. "Don't need a catcher," says Blip. "My bat splits tornados."

Goingsnake spits tobacco juice on the ground. "Okay," he says casually, "but Hope don't throw no tornados."

"He will today," says Blip, practicing his swing. "We're playing against soldiers."

Hope doesn't react or abandon his spittle-lubed snarl, not even for Blip. Not today. Rather, he strides out to the mound with five base-balls in the crook of his left arm. He sets them on the red dirt. Taking the first ball in his right hand, he winds up and fires toward home.

Blip belts it into left field, where centerfielder Nolan Berryhill scrambles after it.

The next pitch is high. Blip fouls it.

Hope winds up again, this time throwing a fastball with a twister's tail that reverses itself as it drops in. Most batters don't even see a seam. But instead of aiming for the ball, Blip calls it to his bat and slams it into tomorrow. Later, when a spectator asks him what happened to the ball, Blip will say he knocked it into the future.

After talking with Ezol that first night, after considering her details—some more lucid than others—I searched the web and found that Carl Laemmle's International Moving Pictures had made what is considered the first film drama about American baseball. I ordered a copy of the film from the Library of Congress. I'd made a career of being able to verify facts. Ezol's stories should be no different. I also needed to prove, at least to myself, that I wasn't suffering from some kind of mental breakdown.

When the film arrived from Washington, D.C., I was stunned. There she was in the final scene, crudely made up to look like a man, playing one of the gravediggers. I knew then that she, a Choctaw woman from the past, a spirit, had told the truth about her experiences and the lives of the Indian baseball players she'd known in Ada. Her information had been correct and, most important to me, verifiable. When she reappeared a couple of weeks later, I was ready. I knew we were going to write the story of the Miko Kings together. She would talk and I'd write. Eventually I realized that I wasn't writing, but merely taking dictation from a woman who wasn't...well, she wasn't *present tense.*

Was she a dream? Perhaps. But she was more than that.

A lost soul? Definitely not lost. She chose to be here with me. And yet I've come to understand that if she isn't present, if I don't stay cloistered with her, the story of Indian Territory baseball and the men who played the game may never be told. So I listen, caught up in a virtual world of her making. We talk of the teams' great victories, their tragic losses and, of course, her philosophy of time.

She is the narrator; I the medium, intermediary, stenographer, and servant to the story. My work as a translator feeds this apparition in my house. To be any good at translation, you have to do a kind of disappearing act. Teach yourself to become invisible by breathing life onto the page, and then exist there, side by side with the words and images. At least for a time.

What became of the Miko Kings—what happened to Ezol Day and the untimely events that brought her to me—are things I could never have imagined or written on my own. Simply put, the voice speaking is my voice, but the voice of this story is hers.

Here is another echo of baseball's childhood
memory in *Anompa Sipokni,* Old Talking Places.

*After the bases are gone*
*After we've all come home*
*Nothing but red dirt in my skivvies*
*My back and ribs is sore*
*May I never go back*
*for another crack at the bat, Honey*
*until the bases are loaded once more.*

# 2

## Indian Territory, As Told by Ezol Day, Postal Clerk and Experimenter of Time

*Ada, Oklahoma, August 1, 2006*

At two a.m., the sky is exceedingly bright as bodies of stars sashay across the heavens. I awaken to my alarm with great anticipation, believing tonight's encounter with Ezol Day will reveal another important clue as to what happened to the Miko Kings and why their story is erased from the historic record. Or at the very least, missing.

I make myself a cup of coffee. Because Ada is a small sleepy town in south central Oklahoma, there is very little light pollution. The early morning air, with little humidity, is completely still. I open the white French doors of my office and slide the screen shut to keep out mosquitoes. For the past six nights we've been working until dawn. I find it hard to stay awake, so I've been making myself go to bed long before dark and wake up early to prepare for her arrival. Because we rarely meet in the other rooms of the house, I've already positioned myself in front of my computer.

And then she appears.

When she first arrives, she recognizes nothing. Her routine is this. She walks across the room and examines all the family pictures hanging on the wall in my office. Her routine behavior makes me realize how I've burdened this room with the past. She stares at each image for a moment, then asks about only one. I tell her the little girl with her arms around the dog is a photograph of my mother, Kit. It has been the same each night. At first, it puzzled me, but I've come to believe that Ezol undergoes a kind of re-entry reunion with the future each time she appears. My office is in the new addition of the house and would not have been there when she was alive. I tell myself this accounts for her strange behavior. Whatever the case, Ezol always shrugs and takes a seat in a nineteenth-century leather wingback chair that I've strategically placed in front of my computer desk. The chair belonged to MourningTree. When I returned from Amman it was the first piece of furniture I had reupholstered, in bordello red, a "period" color from the nineteenth century. I believe the chair helps Ezol settle in.

In the dim light of my office, Ezol's radiant dark brown skin is exactly the same color as her hair. She piles it high into a chignon. Very fashionable at the turn of the nineteenth century. She wears a white linen blouse and a black skirt cinched at the waist with a narrow belt. The sameness of her hair, skin, and eyes makes her appear like one of the photographs hanging on the wall.

"I've been thinking," she says, "this must have been Uncle Henri and Cousin Cora's house. They lived in a house just like this one on West Ninth Street."

"No," I answer. "The land belonged to MourningTree Bolin, my grandmother, and she built the house. This was her allotment, I have the papers to prove it. They're in the safety deposit box in my bank."

Ezol smoothes the hem of her dress. "Documents lie," she says casually. "The Bolins were Choctaws from Tish and they never relocated to Ada."

"Tish" is the way locals refer to Tishomingo, a Chickasaw town thirty miles from Ada. But I know my grandmother's family history and on this point I will not defer, even to a ghost.

"We're not related to the Bolins from Tish. We're the Bolins from Fittstown. Hank Bolin was my grandfather. This house was built on MourningTree's land. Back then, Choctaws didn't always have last names. Grandmother told me this herself. When she married my grandfather, she became MourningTree Bolin. No one else has ever lived in this house or on her land."

Ezol studies me. Her eyes are kind. I like it that she looks directly into my eyes when she wants to make a point. In some ways I think she resembles my grandmother, however, I have to remind myself that loneliness may be coloring my judgment. I've come home but my loved ones are all dead, so whatever resemblance I see in Ezol is just plain longing.

"In 1904," says Ezol, "75,000 white people in Indian Territory applied to the U.S. Dawes Commission for a place on the rolls of the Choctaw and the Chickasaw Nations. Everyone knew if they were accepted on the Dawes Rolls they'd receive a section, or two, of the tribes' allotment lands. Free for the taking. The Dawes Commission admitted them all, but the Cherokees and Choctaws contested the inflated numbers and appealed to the government for a review. It's still pending."

"What is?"

"Identity," she says. "No one will ever know who they really are if they rely on paper identities issued by the federal government. Documents cannot be trusted."

"What about the documents in the mail pouch?" I ask.

Silence.

Ezol looks away, lost in the memories of her time. At least that's how she appears to me. After a long while she picks up the pages I've typed and begins reading aloud:

"Meanwhile in Ada, a Choctaw woman rails against the epidemic of forgers, fraudsters, grafters, and thieves. Finally, she gives birth to a baby with four fully formed front teeth. An editorial in the *Ada Weekly News* suggests that she give her newborn a rifle. Nothing, says the editor, will stop the Indians from being swindled out of their land, or disappearing from the face of the earth. Except a war." She pauses.

"Where did you find this editorial?" Ezol asks, holding the pages in her hand like a writ.

"From a newspaper clipping in the mail pouch. It's from 1904."

Ezol sits erect as a judge and continues reading aloud from the first chapter of our book.

Nobody said it was pretty here, but it's demanding. Like a beehive—full of activity. The photograph of the Miko Kings fits in nicely next to the pictures of Ada's four hotels, three banks, four cotton gins, fire depot, glass plant, and flourmill huffing powdery wheat dust and emphysema into the air.

Of course, peculiar rules begin to emerge in Ada, the town whose trajectory is on a collision course with fancy. The most widely criticized ordinance says no female under eighteen can be hypnotized, and no male under twenty-one can be hypnotized without the consent of a parent or guardian.

In 1904, Choctaw entrepreneur Henri Day begins building a baseball park in Ada, and a baseball team called the Miko Kings. He also has plans for an all Indian-owned baseball league.

A skunk farm is also established near Ada that same year. E.P. Dowd, a wealthy New York furrier, wants to breed "champagne blondes" and bets that their fur will be as valuable as mink in the coming decade. Dowd puts his money where his ideas are. His headquarters are in Civets (named for the French *civette,* or skunk), a town northeast of Pauls Valley. The following week, a local trapper named Sam Lewis, who's never worn anything but a cowhide jacket, mulls over the notion of wearing skunk. "I'm willing to give it a try," he tells Charlie Catcher, the reporter for the *Ada Weekly News.*

Lewis has been hired as foreman to oversee operations at Dowd's Skunk Farm. He assures Adans that the twenty-acre farm (as it's called) will be enclosed with a cement wall, making it thoroughly escape-proof.

"You gotta get them little stinkers cut off by the fourth week, or else. My helper at the farm, an Indian kid named Hope Little Leader, is learning the hard way," laughs Lewis. "Just last week we soaked him in a tub of tomato juice to get the stench off, but little good it did him. Skunk wrangling takes time. We're gonna give him another go at it."

Just about every adult has survived a spell of typhoid fever. If a yellow flag flies outside a house, it means the family has contracted smallpox. Dozens die in December 1904, but Ada birthrates continue to soar.

Still others die as criminals. Take the recent newspaper story, "The Gunslingers from Vici Came, Saw, Were Conquered in Ada!" Jim Harris, Willie Bailey, and Jeff Woodall, all from Vici in northwestern Dewey County (named for the Latin *veni, vidi, vici*), got into a brawl over a floozy at Pud Kyser's joint on Broadway last Friday. Two were shot dead. Woodall's throat was cut almost from ear to ear. The newspaper reports that Woodall is probably mortally wounded.

The following week, Deputy Marshal Bob Nester makes a daylight raid to halt criminal activity at Kyser's. As he goes in the front door, three gamblers jump out the second story window. Nester, somewhat chagrined at their daring getaway, fires a few intimidating shots as he shouts, "If you rabble-rousers ever run from me again, I'll shoot to kill!"

Unfortunately, as the town grows so does corruption. A federal judge in Ardmore gets wind of the sleaze in Ada and issues twenty-one warrants against the town's most prominent citizens, alleging that they're selling land belonging to the Chickasaw Nation. (Issuing fraudulent deeds is not a new practice in Indian Territory.) The judge sends newly appointed U.S. Marshal Basil Bennett to Ada with the warrants. However, just as soon as Bennett arrives in town, the warrants mysteriously disappear. Within a month, Bennett is elected Ada's town marshal. Commerce continues unabated.

Every Tuesday at noon, members of the Commercial Club gather at the Harris Hotel to hear a lecture on morality, temperance, or both. But Thursday afternoon, most of the male members of the club gallop their horses out of Ada and ride hard for thirteen miles into Pottawatomie Country. They pass dozens of blackjack trees, green crater-shaped hills, and old Pottawatomie ladies napping in front of dilapidated shacks, their blue and red blankets wrapped loosely around them. But the men are blind to their surroundings. They're lost in the details of turning straw into gold. Gambling fever will do that to men on a quest. The riders slow down at the muddy South Canadian River and cautiously mosey around the drifting quicksand cavities, then pick up the pace at a tree stump sign on the north side of the river that reads "Corner Saloon Open. Two Miles."

Tom Bobbitt, the Corner Saloon's most recent co-owner, is a belching, wind-passing box of a man. He goes out of his way to disavow the other Bobbitts in Ada, calling them ramrodding Biblists. When Bobbitt moved up from Texas to go into business with the Corner Saloon's owner, Bill Connors, gamblers from as far away as St. Louis celebrated.

For Bobbitt, betting on Indians is like betting on horses. "They're both commodities," he says to Charlie Catcher, who later quotes him in the newspaper. Bobbitt and the other gamblers guzzle whiskey, banter back and forth over the teams, and relive each inning they've bet on.

By 1905, the counter behind the bar is crammed with jars full of clippings about National and American League teams collected from newspapers as far away as Ohio's *Cleveland Plain Dealer*. Saloon patrons bring the clippings to Bobbitt so he can maintain accurate records. On Fridays Bobbitt posts league standings, the starting line-ups, statistics, and the odds on a large blackboard behind the counter. His betting list includes "Southpaws," "Three-fingered players," "Weaklings," and "Sackers."

Other incidentals for sale at the Corner Saloon are not mentioned in polite company. Such as women and little boys.

Then there's Dr. Price's Special Wheat Cure for Gonorrhea, and potency powders like Spanish Fly and Elk Horn Crush. So far, the Chinese railroad workers are the only ones buying the Elk Horn Crush that promises in tiny but legible print "to create a mighty force in men."

The Corner Saloon's policy is completely democratic about who can purchase shots of whiskey, remedies for fornicators, or time with the half-naked prostitutes living around back. Tom Bobbitt says he doesn't care who does what to whom as long as they all pay him a share of the arrangements. For anyone who misunderstands the policy, Bobbitt wears a thirty-three-inch-long Light Cavalry saber sheathed on his belt, and a Colt Six-Shooter is strapped on his right leg. He is rumored to have stabbed as many as four men in one night when they had forgotten the rules.

"I only kill to protect the safety of our patrons," says Bobbitt. "That's the secret of our success."

Over the next two years, money pours into Ada. The city's motto becomes "Nothing is too big or too good for Ada." Miko Kings' popularity seems to know no boundaries. Even the Katy Restaurant, next to the train depot, stays open twenty-four hours, seven days a week, to serve the throngs of fans who come to watch the Indian baseball games.

But change does finally come to Indian Territory. The land shudders at the thought. When time slips out of its boundaries, everything falls every which way. Wild horses leap into the air and whinny. Panthers cry like babies in the streets, along with the sorry gamblers and drunkards who imagine games that never were. Although no one now can clearly recall the Miko Kings, it is here where the image, the reflection, the photograph of the greatest Indian baseball team still exists.

Now time opens like a coffin.


At last Ezol Day stops reading. "The story is not exactly right, but it's not wrong either," she says. "How did you find out about the Corner Saloon?"

"The records at the Oklahoma Historical Society," I say. "It must have been infamous, because it was repeatedly mentioned as a headquarters for gamblers, prostitutes, and their friends. I read that Bobbitt and Connors supposedly paid the local sheriffs hush money when they had to 'shoot at' a patron, which was apparently code for killing someone."

Ezol nods and reflects on what I've said.

"I didn't know about the uses for elk horn, but men always rode out there to place their bets on the baseball games. That much was common knowledge. Bobbitt claimed that he was the best thing that ever happened to the Miko Kings. He once told Uncle Henri that without the gamblers, Miko Kings' ballpark would go under."

"Was he right?"

She stares past me and doesn't answer. Her eyes seem to be directed outwards, locked toward some distant memory.

"How did you know Hope was once a skunk farmer?" she asks.

"I found the abstract and title for Dowd's Skunk Farm among some papers at the historical society. Hope Little Leader was listed as one of the farm hands."

At that moment we hear a fire truck race down the street. Ezol goes to the window and for a long while she observes the darkness in silence. Finally she says, "The circus lion is burned up in his cage. A black bear named Bobby suffocates from the smoke. Blinded first, he feels the fire singe the rest of him. Only the peacocks survive. But there was something about the way the people came the very next day—all dressed up in their finest clothes. Even Cora came to help clean up the debris and carry off the dead."

Ezol turns around and smiles regretfully. "Choctaws and Chickasaws are renowned for their ability to rebuild. It was their reaction to the fire that helped me understand that there is honor in all things. We seemed to manifest nature itself, as re-creators," she says softly. "Chaos and destruction serve a purpose, you know."

I nod absentmindedly. I've learned to keep a running list of things to research, so I keep a yellow notepad next to my computer. I write, "Circus fire in Ada—what year?"

Ezol walks again over to my wall of photographs and straightens the picture of my mother.

"That's Kit," I say hesitantly, "my mother. She died a week after I was born."

"Kit," she says, touching the frame again. "I like her name. She looks like a friend of mine."

I don't know what to say, so I smile weakly. "In a way, the whole of Indian Territory was made up of imposters," says Ezol. "The difficulty for self-invented people is that they must always reconcile what they were back then with who they are now. Bo Hash and Justina

Maurepas were imposters. They invented themselves again and again, especially Justina. Their behaviors wreaked havoc with their loved ones, but Justina was my dear friend. She understood me, and she never laughed at my equations and my notions about time. I will always honor her for that."

"Who were they?" I ask. "You've never mentioned Bo and Justina before."

"Two more people important to the story I am telling."

Another present-day sound interrupts us. This time a garbage truck has pulled up in the alley behind my house. Although it's still dark, dawn is approaching. Ezol goes to investigate and stands at the French doors that open onto the backyard. I'm interested to find out what modern sounds can mean to someone from the past. She watches from the doorway while a sanitation worker tosses glass bottles into a bin of his truck. I note that she's curious about all things unfamiliar. She lingers a moment longer at the back door, then returns.

"Interesting," she says, finally.

"What is?" I ask.

"The workman outside."

"We recycle now," I say.

"We did too," she says. "Back then, they were called scavengers."

I assume she means that Indians left their refuse for the buzzards, or other carrion-feeders, but I add "scavenger" to my list of things to research.

"Ada is an event in which I isolate myself now and again," she says. "The circus that came to town, the moving picture producer, the fire, the ballgames—they all happened here. But then, everything, even the farthest universe, has already happened. They're stories that travel now as captured light in someone else's telescope. No?"

Ezol reaches for the crystal pitcher of water on a small table next to her. She pours water into one of the glasses but, as usual, never touches it. I've come to realize she likes to fill the goblet with water, underscoring a vital truth. Water is life.

I pause and think for a moment. I want to say that I lived in an area of the world where water is a precious gift. I once walked fifteen miles in the baking heat of the Nabataean desert with a group of Bedouin women. The women never took a drink of water until after dusk, when the sheep were bedded down for the night. I also think of explaining that my stories now appear in the virtual world of online magazines. The captured light of a computer screen. But since those are not the discussions she's interested in, I shrug.

"There are some hundred thousand million galaxies in our known universe," I say. "I've read that superstring theorists believe there are ten dimensions in spacetime, and that humans only see a meager slice of reality."

She frowns.

I dig deeper, trying to recall what, if anything, my grandmother told me about Choctaw medicine. Not much, I'm afraid. Of course medicine people have always told stories about their vision quests and journeys to other dimensions. Most white people, academics, Christians, even some Indians, dismiss these stories as "myths." But I'm talking to someone who existed—or exists—in another dimension, and I'm intimidated by my own ignorance. I say I don't know.

"We will come back to that," she says. "I am speaking now about Ada, the boomtown. The railroads have brought in so many newcomers, we don't know where they are going to live."

"Who?" I ask.

"Adans. Indians. People," says Ezol.

"But that time has passed," I say. "Most of Ada's merchants went bankrupt a long time ago. Pushed out of business by progress. Large multinational corporations like Wal-Mart and..."

Ezol takes a deep breath, and I realize that she is dictating again. I place my fingers on the keyboard.

"Ready," I say, as I type.

"Adans *were* intent on keeping the streets clean. The cafés in Ada, and the hotels, *were* open day and night," she says curtly, pausing to press her fingertips on her forehead.

"Verb tenses," she says impatiently. "I was right about analyzing language as the way into my theorem of time. The laws of physics do not distinguish between past and present. Neither does the Choctaw language, at least not in the way that English does. Choctaw verbs have a much broader application, which shades the meaning in ways that English verbs cannot. Take for instance the word *chifitokchaya*."

"I don't know what it means."

"Run and live," she says.

"That's a hard one to imagine," I say.

"Not if you're a batter on third," says Ezol. "Now what do you see when I say *chifitokchaya*?"

"A baseball player running for home plate!" I say, excited.

She smiles. "Choctaw words are tools. They form equations, much the same as geometry," she says confidently. "Geometry may be guided by facts, but those facts are ultimately the choice, or consent, of a specific group. Language, rules of grammar, and meaning are the agreement of a particular group based on their practiced experience. I theorized that Choctaws didn't have the same experiences with time as those of Europeans because we speak differently. This is revealed in our vast differences in verb usage. What the Choctaws spoke of, they saw. Experienced."

I stop typing for a moment and study her mannerisms. The delicate customs she keeps for herself. I think she's decidedly patrician for a Choctaw who first came to Ada in 1900 from the Good Land Indian Orphanage. What I have been able to piece together about her life comes from a Christmas letter in the mail pouch from a minister at Good Land. She was the niece of Henri Day, born in Doaksville in 1879 to Ellen Day, Henri's sister. Ezol remained at Good Land until she was twenty-one. I think it's strange that she didn't come to live with her uncle and cousin until she was grown.

In 1905 Ezol Day wrote an article entitled "Moving Bodies in

Choctaw Space," in which she argued that two systems of thought, Choctaw and English, are in conflict over "time." She posited that universal time in space could not exist because there are no universal verb tenses. She based her hypothesis on language theory, and concluded that time must flow at different rates for English speakers and for tribal peoples. Her paper is elegantly reasoned, addressing fundamental questions around Choctaw expressions of space and time. She was writing at the same time as Albert Einstein, but probing the dimension of cultures, as well as of time and space. I wonder how she was able to do it with only a boarding school education.

"Are you tired?" she asks, pointing to the keyboard. "You've stopped typing."

"No, I was just thinking," I say, placing my hands on the keys. "I'm ready."

Ezol Day looks at me as if she's studying misfortune. Then she begins dictating.

"Consider this. *Okchamali* is the Choctaw word for both blue and green," she says. "Its roots appear in the Choctaw word *okchanya,* meaning 'alive.' Now, where did our people originate? Answer: a world of blue sky and green swamplands, a watery place. So perhaps *okchamali* relates to 'place' as 'alive.'"

"Or 'lived,' as in past tense?" I ask.

She shakes her head passionately. "Not past tense, exactly," she says. "*Okchamali* could be a description of a place name of a primeval epoch when the sky and the sea were so close that there was almost no atmosphere in between. In Choctaw it is the subtle shading, the intensity and grayness, the dullness or brilliance of a thing that determines how it is spoken of. Our language marked the dullness of the sky *in that place* at that particular time. If it were the primordial beginning of the earth, the visible eye would not have been able to distinguish the shimmering 'above' or 'below.' *Okchamali* then becomes a descriptive remnant, the color of a time that the ancient Choctaws experienced or, most likely, knew of. *Okchamali,* then, signifies *life.*"

"How is that possible?" I ask.

"Verbs," she answers, pushing a wisp of hair off her face. She continues rapidly, obviously in her element. "Some Choctaw words are tools, in the same way that numbers are tools. We have evidence in our language that our people experienced other dimensions through our use of particles and verbs which attend to specific movements in and out of spacetime. I asked myself why this was so. The logic I used in my Choctaw theorem of time is built around verbs. I questioned why we should expect our ancestors to synchronize their time with our modern clocks, which are set and reset by the political whims of English speakers."

"We shouldn't!" I answer boldly.

She scrutinizes me.

"I mean it," I say sincerely. "I've been living abroad for so long that what little I once knew about Choctaw language I've forgotten. But it will come back to me. Besides, I don't really understand physics, the etymology of our language, or moving bodies in space. What does all this have to do with the Miko Kings and baseball?"

"Everything, Lena! After I understood that there might be other spacetime terms embedded in our language, I looked for them in plants that contain sacred geometric expressions. I studied the patterns in our stomp dances and baseball games. Words make equations the same way that numbers connect us to other dimensions and to *okchamali.*"

She so rarely calls me by name that I'm caught off guard. Also, I've never heard an Indian talk about a baseball game or a stomp dance as a mathematical equation. Although I admit I've been away from home for a long time.

"Base-and-ball," says Ezol, "was a game that was played on every ancient square ground in the southeast. It had two intersecting lines that crossed at the mound where the pitcher stood. Natives played variations of the game all over North and South America long before white people ever arrived in the New World. From the mound, a pitcher was the embodiment of the center pole that could access the Middle, Upper, and Lower Worlds."

"Did I mention that I once played ball?" I ask.

"When?"

"1970. The same year Grandpa Hank died. I was eleven. Grandmother enrolled me in the Choctaw little league softball program. Every Saturday morning she'd drive us to McAlester so I could play for the Little Chahtas, a girls' fast-pitch team."

Now Ezol looks uncomfortable. "What position?"

"Left field."

"Were you a good hitter?"

"No. I have no athletic abilities and I didn't learn a thing about the game. That summer I nursed a black eye, four sprained fingers, and I was knocked out cold by a fly ball." I smile. "It's been at least thirty-five years and I can still hear Grandmother shouting from the bleachers, *Lena, use both hands!*"

Suddenly Ezol sits erect in her chair. "That's right," she says happily. "Use both hands."

"I'm sure you've heard that a million times."

Her bright smile fades quickly. "Well no, not exactly."

Something I said registered with her, an unpleasant memory perhaps. But when she won't say more I begin typing, hoping she'll come back to it. "After fast-pitch season ended," I say, "Grandmother said the blood had just run out on me. She said everyone else in the family loved to play ball except me, and I was a total failure."

"You weren't a failure, it just wasn't your game," she says softly. "Indians invented all kinds of ball games. Some are for fun. Other games, like stickball, are good training for warriors. Base-and-ball helped with diplomacy between tribes. But not everyone is meant to be a ball player. You've traveled all over the world and even learned to speak Arabic? That shows you are very accomplished. And I suspect Arabic has a different verb tense system from English."

"Yes," I say. "They also have a different notion of time...*Arab time.*"

We both smile.

"Were you lonely living so far from home?" she asks.

"Yes," I say, yawning and standing to stretch my legs. "But I didn't realize how isolated I felt until I was home. In November 2005, when one of my close friends was killed, that was really the beginning of the end of my life in Amman. He was working at the Days Inn in Amman when a terrorist bomb exploded. Then, in the spring of this year, I heard a strange voice during the call to prayer and I began chanting aloud with it.

Allahu Akbar. *The time has come to return home.*
Allahu Akbar. *The time has come to return home.*
Allahu Akbar. *The time has come to return home.*
Allahu Akbar. *The time has come to return home.*

Ezol looks down at her lap. "You say you chanted the words four times and then you came home?"

For a moment neither of us speaks. I think I understand what she's getting at. I spoke of home and now I'm home.

"Something like that," I say. "Three planes, a bus, a car ride, and *Wa'llahe,* I finally returned home."

"What did you say in Arabic?"

"'By God.' But it's never uttered in polite company."

Ezol smiles at me like a proud parent. "Do you still miss your friend?"

"Yes," I say, looking away. "I do."

Briefly I consider asking her if we're related. We must be. She seems to read me like a book. Besides, why else would her papers have ended up inside the walls of my grandmother's house? My stern conviction a few hours ago—that I knew my family's history—now seems childish. Even ridiculous. I make a note to go to the bank and open my safety deposit box and look at the land title and abstract for Grandmother's house. Perhaps the Day family is mentioned.

I decide to change the subject before she asks me something else personal. "You know, just about everyone in America believes Abner

Doubleday invented baseball."

"A myth," says Ezol, touching the water glass absentmindedly, then pushing it away. "How plausible is it that white people, who live by the clock and sword, would invent a game without time, one that must be played counter-clockwise?"

Something she says triggers an incident I'd completely forgotten. "Grandmother and I went to an *Alikchi,* a Choctaw doctor, for a healing ceremony," I say, excitedly. "It was the summer of 1969. I remember the year because I was ten and could swim in the adult pool at Glenwood Park."

Ezol seems to be withdrawing, her whole presence elongating and softening, as she does when leaving our sessions.

"What's wrong?" I ask. "Where are you going?"

"Nowhere," she says, coming back to the present. "Please go on. The year is 1969. What happened?"

"Grandmother drove us to Tannehill, just outside of McAlester. After awhile, tornado clouds blew in. The winds were howling like a freight train. Grandmother and I had to hold on to a big cottonwood tree to keep from blowing away. I was terrified, but the *Alikchi* kept on pitching his ax into the ground until the earth opened up a large crater. Then, as the winds died down, he walked counter-clockwise around and around the crater. After awhile the clouds disappeared and the sky was blue again."

"Who was the ceremony for?" she asks.

"I can't remember. I was so scared I guess I blocked it out until now."

"Call it to you!" she snaps. "Call the memory to you, Lena! Who was the ceremony for? You must know."

I nod and promise I'll try, but I'm sure Grandmother never told me.

Ezol presses me. "What happened to the crater that the *Alikchi* opened up?"

"It disappeared," I say, feeling uneasy again.

Ezol's color returns and she speaks persuasively. "Embedded in these rituals and games are mathematical codes that harness cosmic forces. You witnessed it for yourself."

"The *Alikchi* didn't use a mathematical formula, I know that."

"How do you know that?"

"I just know."

"Choctaw language doesn't distinguish 'science' from 'the sacred,'" she says. "The *Alikchi* might be surprised to know he couldn't be a mathematical physicist, since he could split the clouds and open a passage to another time and space."

"I didn't mean to imply that he was primitive," I say, defensively. "He just didn't use math."

"Why do you keep saying that?" asks Ezol. "Indians in North and South America built cosmic observatories in the form of mounds and pyramids, very complicated structures that require geometry. A stomp dance and a baseball game mimic natural phenomena, such as tornado winds, that are counter-clockwise. Why can't you believe that the *Alikchi* knew how to interact with the chaos?"

"Listen," I say curtly. "I may not know Choctaw language, but I know that the *Alikchi* was not a scientist and he was not a god."

"So you do remember more than you let on!"

"I don't know...yes. Maybe...I don't know."

Ezol smiles. "I thought so."

Silence.

"But I still don't think baseball is a sacred game," I say, still defensive.

"Don't confuse our ancient game with the one that's been assimilated into America's consciousness," she snaps. "Remember that the first thing whites did during their civil war was exclude blacks from playing on their baseball teams. Later they excluded Jews. But base-and-ball, *our game,* was created so that we could include everyone. We played the game to collaborate with other tribes, the stars, and with the great mystery. The game is *past time* for a reason."

Again she's pulled me up short. I mouth the words *past time* and let the concept wash over me. "There's no time limit in baseball."

"Or any other Native game," she says sharply. "Why is that?"

Silence.

"But you are right about our *Alikchi*," says Ezol, her voice softening as she touches the glass of water. "They are much more like healers working in collaboration with the earth's mathematical systems. That's the power Hope Little Leader had."

"What do you mean?"

"With his hands Hope could collaborate with nature. Hope was special, and Blip and the others knew it. They loved him for it, but it's because of his recklessness that we all ended up..." Ezol pauses and tears well up in her eyes, "...forgotten. Like your memory of the healing ceremony. If that isn't bad enough..."

I finish her sentence, "...you're telling your story to someone who has cared very little about baseball. Someone who never once considered how an *Alikchi* shifts time and space, or how a physicist reckons them. All I've got is a belief that you are here with me now."

Ezol shakes her head. "You have a little more than that," she says.

At moments like this I have the strangest sensation that we're mirror images of one another, that we both seem to be searching through our pasts for answers.

Ezol shifts uncomfortably in her chair and then stands up. As she walks around the room she touches every object.

"Time is like a majestic dance," she says. "Observe how I can step forward or backwards or sideways and form multiple patterns that intersect."

"Which is how you're here with me now, but also in another time and space?"

"Something like that," she says a little wistfully. "Your time and my time are two distinct patterns, but they intersect. That's why I'm here."

I remind her that along with the photograph of the Miko Kings, I have a copy of Carl Laemmle's film that she and the ballplayers appeared in. I also have a letter from the U.S. Patent Office rejecting her paper on Choctaw time.

"The envelope is postmarked November 1, 1907," I say. "A record of you and your theory does exist."

Ezol looks aggrieved, as if she didn't know about the rejection letter. How could she not know? Even in 1907 she must have known it was impossible to patent ideas.

"I found a 1904 newspaper clipping about the Crazy Snake delegation going off to Washington D.C. without asking permission of the Commissioner of Indian Affairs, Captain A. Clarke Tonnor. The article said Henri Day sent the Crazy Snake delegation enough money to return to Ada. But so far I've found very little else about players and their families."

"The money actually came from the Four Mothers Society, a group that tried to stop the allotting of our lands. Uncle Henri was covering for them. In the first year, 1904, almost half of our baseball ticket sales were going to the Four Mothers Society. Aunt Emma, Uncle Henri's mother, was one of the leaders until she died in 1906."

Ezol walks over to the desk and begins writing on my yellow notepad. "The only photograph of Hope that I liked was taken in Hampton, Virginia, three years before I met him," she says. "He had a look of innocence, the look of not knowing the power that would come for him. I suspect the picture is still there if you go look for it."

I smile meekly as I read over her list.

"You better get started on your research," she quips. "I can see you have a lot of holes in your education."

At the top of the page, she's written three mathematical equations, "John Lennon," and "Four Mothers Society." I can't imagine why she wants me to research the Beatles. At the bottom of the page she's scribbled, "Find out what happened to John. Also, you can look for Hope Little Leader's records at Hampton Normal School for Blacks and Indians."

But before Ezol disappears, I ask her about Hope's pitches. "I don't know anything about pitching. How did he make the ball reverse itself?"

"Have you ever seen Michelangelo's painting of how God created Adam?"

"Yes," I say.

Ezol wiggles the fingers on her right hand. "It's all in the velocity of the fingertips, no?" She gestures toward the window. "Dawn arrives," she says. "See how the moon scorches away in a cloud of light and steam. Gone in the blink of an eye. Of course, if there were people on the moon they could not discern this event because we see it from our vantage point on earth."

"So…" I think out loud, my head spinning, "the *Alikchi* knew how to shift his vision so he could see everything all at once?"

Again Ezol smiles as if I were a small child that had just amused her. She places her hands on the small of her back and stretches first to the left, then right. A strange gesture for a spirit. Then she walks around the desk to stand beside my chair and studies the computer screen.

"Captured light?" she asks.

I nod in agreement.

"Do all the colors of the visible spectrum appear here?"

"I'm not sure," I say. "Maybe a million shades or variations of colors are…"

*"Shush,"* she says. "Please type the names of the men who played for Miko Kings and the positions they played. I want to see them appear in the light. Later, I'll tell you everything that happened. All I know about space and time and baseball as medicine. But first, type their names."

She stands completely still, as if overtaken by a memory marked with grief. I don't think she even breathes.

**Miko Kings**

1) Centerfield: Nolan Berryhill, Creek

2) Left Field: Blip Bleen, Chickasaw-Choctaw

3) Second Base: Isom Joel, Choctaw

4) Right Field: Oscar Pickens, Chickasaw

5) Catcher: Albert "Batteries" Goingsnake, Cherokee

6) Third Base: Napoleon Bonaparte, Choctaw

7) First Base: Lucius Mummy, Mississippi Choctaw

8) Shortstop: Theo Porter, Seminole-Creek

9) Pitcher: Hope Little Leader, Choctaw

She gently touches the screen where Blip's name appears, as if lamenting his bruised body after a particularly tough series. A loss. When she's this close, I can see the large blue-green veins that run along the back of her hand like rivers on a map. How is it possible for a spirit to also be flesh and blood?

Ezol smiles down at me. "Blip once said he was 'Chick-Choc,'" she says softly. "Then he would do something squinty with his eyes—and I would always laugh."

She continues gazing into the screen beyond his name, locked into a landscape of light, farther away than the farthest universe, toward all our lives in Indian Territory.

And I type.

Here too is another echo of baseball's childhood
memory in *Anompa Sipokni,* Old Talking Places.

Freedom smoked from my fingers, he says, riding the
    rails bound for home.
How long were your fingers? asks the Hobo.
Like this.
And your arms?
Like this.
Imagine that!

# 3
## The Bases Are Loaded
### Ada, Oklahoma, September 16, 1969

Someone is playing the same song over and over.

*Because the world is round, it turns me on*
*Because the world is round, Ah*
*Because the wind is high, it blows my mind*
*Because the wind is high, Ah*
*Love is old, love is new*
*Love is all, love is you*

The melody echoes down the long gray halls of the Elms Nursing Home in Ada and circles high above his head like vague sightings of wind. Hope Little Leader knows something about the paths of prairie wind and the influence it can have on a baseball. A good pitcher must make friends with the cross currents of summer. Like a woman, the wind can become jealous and send a stiff gust to tear your shirt off if it's ignored for too long.

He listens to the tender reverie as it repeats again on the phonograph. The young men love the world so round, the sky so blue—that's how he once felt. He looks skyward; a white ceiling of clouds is above him. Just then, the red ball that his uncle Ahojebo gave him is in his eye. Ahojebo used to twirl his arm so fast that when he set the ball free it flew *up, up, up* into the heavens and disappeared. How did the singers know that his uncle's feat always made him cry? Hope rolls on his side; at least he thinks it's his side. A spider walks across the flat surface of the wall. They're roommates and he's comforted by her presence. He can always find her in *yakni kula,* a dug out place underground, where they put him every time he's captured for trying to run away.

*Because the wind is high...*

That's what he once said to her. She says that he seduced her with his stories of winds. Of how his grandfather could split tornados. *Because the wind is high, an Alikchi must split it at the roots.*

Hope steadies himself for another long visit with her, for their former life together to emerge out of the past. He has infinite patience, boarding school taught him that much. Once he waited four days and nights for a single blade of grass to spring up out of the dirt walls of his prison cell at Hampton Normal School for Blacks and Indians.

He searches the wall for the spider and locates her just as she reaches the sky. Hope watches as she fastens a thread onto a nebulous cloud, swings off with the help of the invisible wind, and pays out silk as she descends. She is wafted for many miles until caught unaware by something unseen.

*Ah.*

The older Indian boys in his class make fun of her behind her back because she is so stiff in her manner and never smiles. But Hope has a special name for her. He recalls every detail of her delicate body. Her hair is slick black like the leather of his tight new shoes. Her lips are creased like the segments of an orange, and when she daubs a little oil through her coarse hair and pulls it into a stiff bun, she looks much older than eighteen. Dressed in her dark maroon skirt and high-buttoned bodice, she reminds him of the tiny wooden statue he's seen in the reverend's office. When she writes the strange marks on the school's blackboard, her husky voice purrs low and dangerous like an undernourished panther. Rather than concentrate on what the young teacher's aid is saying about ciphering, he pretends she's tracing those lines from the blackboard all over his body. She is what his uncle would call *shali ninak,* night addiction.

At Hampton Normal School for Blacks and Indians, the two races are not supposed to mix. Reverend Clark, the school's principal, never talks of begetting and mixing, however. He talks about religion, original sin, and the importance of learning civilized ways in order to advance the Indian race.

These talks do not matter to Hope. While he's locked inside *yakni kula* he can clearly imagine his true love's face, with its thick eyebrows and fat lashes, her smooth dusky skin. Dusky Long-Gone Girl, that's what he calls her when he whispers her name in his prayers.

He stretches out on the narrow cot and softly sings the Borrow Money Song:

> *He-ya-ha-bi-yaha-ho wiya ho wiya ho*
> *Ooo-oo-o I'm gonna borrow some money*
> *Ooo-oo-o I'm gonna borrow some money*
> *I'm gonna borrow some money.*

Tears stream down Hope's cheeks. "I'm gonna borrow some money and marry Dusky Long-Gone Girl." He blots his eyes dry with the sleeve of his boarding school uniform.

Somewhere, amid memories that wouldn't exist if time didn't occasionally move back and forth, Hope hears the pop of Blip Bleen's fly ball as it careens overhead past the brand-new ballpark fence, past the tall prairie grass that lies just beyond centerfield and into the great blue beyond.

"It's a goner!" shouts Albert Goingsnake. "That oughta give the Seventh Cavalrymen something to worry about!"

Centerfielder Nolan Berryhill runs after Blip's fly ball into the stiff brown prairie grass that's as tall as a house by mid-September.

"Forget it," yells Hope. "It's way past yonder!"

Hope looks proudly across the Miko Kings ballpark. For the past two weeks nearly everyone in Ada has volunteered something to beautify the diamond and park in preparation for the Twin Territories Series. The ladies of Ada's Sorosis Club even planted a bed of multicolored flowers around the concession stand. Five thousand people are expected to attend the nine-game series that pits the Miko Kings, winners of the Indian Territory League, against Fort Sill's Seventh Cavalrymen, winners of the Oklahoma Territory League.

As Hope's team gathers in their dugout before the start of the first game, first baseman Lucius Mummy nudges him. "Where do you suppose all these folks are coming from?" he asks.

"From all across Indian Territory and Oklahoma Territory," says Blip, putting on his ballcap. "Trainloads of folks. After the game's over, people'll most likely head over to the circus. With all those circus torches going on Main Street, they could send the whole town up in smoke."

Goingsnake winks at Lucius as he hurriedly tucks in his game shirt. "Forget the torches," he says. "There's fire in my belly! There's fire in my hands! Sing hallelujah, brothers, and tell'um on September 16, 1907, catcher Albert "Batteries" Goingsnake was so hot that even his catcher's mitt was smoking!"

"*Whooee-e,* that's some powerful brag," laughs Blip.

"You bet!" says Albert.

His teammates chuckle as a wagonload of Cavalrymen rolls through the far west entrance of the Miko Kings' ballpark. The sound of clanking wheels, an occasional horse whinny, and the voices of children running alongside the wagon grows louder as the soldiers approach the field. Today's headline in the *Ada Weekly News* read: *Cavalry Vows to Avenge Little Big Horn!*

None of the Indian ballplayers will admit they're afraid of what the soldiers might do if they lose the nine-game series. As far as most Indians are concerned, the Seventh Cavalry are dangerous sore losers. Since Custer's Last Stand, they've tried to kill every Indian on the continent. They harassed Chief Joseph and the Nez Perce Indians until they surrendered in 1877. Then came the massacre of innocent women and children at Wounded Knee in 1890. And now they have Geronimo locked up in their stockade.

Fort Sill's baseball manager, Major General Shelby Thornton, is a first-rate Indian killer—his most famous military campaign was Wounded Knee. As the wagon pulls up to the grandstands, Thornton dismounts from a dark red stallion and the men wait for his signal to take their places in the visiting team's dugout.

Throughout the season, the Oklahoma Territory League has been in a three-way dogfight between the Kaw City Kids, the Mullhall Giants, and the Seventh Cavalrymen. Although the Seventh Cavalry have been officially moved out of Fort Sill this year, there was never any question of whether Thornton and his men would come to play for the championship title.

When the Cavalry's pitching fell off, a young hurler named Private Jack Stout was transferred to Fort Sill. He lobbed an amazing twenty wins, helping them capture the Oklahoma Territory title. Stout is supported by veteran lefty Lieutenant Colonel Paddy McKnight, the Seventh Cavalry's relief pitcher. Thornton knows the reputation of the Miko Kings, and he saw them pound the Kaw City Kids 7-0 late in the season. He senses they are a team of the future. Men who are significantly younger than his squad, and they're paid big money to play ball. As much as seventy-five dollars a month during the season.

Henri repeatedly claims that even though the U.S. government pays soldiers "coolie wages," the Seventh Cavalry would play against Indians for free, because, as he says, "We're the goddamn hostiles. But 'Pride goeth before destruction, and a haughty spirit before a fall'…every time. Proverbs 16:18. Don't worry boys, we will prevail. This is our moment in history!"

Hope thinks Henri is a little cuckoo. He quotes the Bible in one breath and curses God in the next. Hope asks himself why he listens to a bicycle-riding Choctaw who's sworn off horses. But for all Henri's "goddamn this" and "goddamn that," he's right about the soldiers. They'd play against Indians for free.

He watches as another mass of white people arrive at the ballpark. The Katy must have emptied out another load of town folks from Purcell. A dozen or so horse-drawn carriages trot toward the grandstands.

"Miko Kings is the one thing the Naholla can't destroy!" shouts Hope to the spectators coming into the ballpark. In spite of himself, he often quotes Henri or Blip.

Hope surveys the sky. The west wind is kicking up the dust. Countless clouds pursue the edge of the horizon. He tosses a ball in the air, testing the wind, as he considers the team's future. The major leagues will have to take notice if the Miko Kings win the series. He looks around the ballfield and then up into the sky again. The afternoon light is good—easy on the eyes. The game is beginning to feel like a memory, perhaps because he's played it so often in his mind. What was it Justina said last night at supper? "Memories congenial as food"? He has no idea what she meant, but it sounded almost like a song. Hope tucks his glove under his arm and concentrates on moving his fingers. They're stiffer than usual today.

Blip slaps him on the back and the two men stand like brothers beneath the sun's autumn rays. "Looks like the Cavalrymen even brought their cannons. Scott and Benteen are the best hitters I've ever seen. So much is gonna depend on you in the next few games."

"You worried?" asks Hope.

"Nope."

"Liar," says Hope.

Both men grin.

Even before Hope came to play for the Miko Kings, he deeply respected Blip's passionate approach to hitting the ball. When he was still working the skunk farm, he'd taken the train over to McAlester to watch Blip Bleen play. Blip is a man who lives the game. He's always honing his swing. Making slight adjustments to where he places his hands on the bat, or the way he stands at the plate. If Blip falls into a hitting slump, he always asks Albert to help him correct his swing.

As a player-manager, Blip is gifted at inspiring the men. He tells them to imagine the plays *before* they happen. Blip studies the way each player uses his body on the field, then coaches to their strengths. He's told Hope that he must have inherited *tikba,* a power, from the original ball players who play nightly among the stars. Blip said he knows enough to stay out of the way of such powers—and that Hope better use them wisely.

A photographer from the nearby town of Stonewall has arranged to take some pictures. Following the photographer's instructions, the team falls into place. Batters in the front row. Catcher, shortstop, and pitcher in the middle. Fielders on the ends. Blip is on the left, with his hand gripped on the knob of the bat. Henri Day, Lonnie Johns, and

Bo Hash stand in the back row. "Make it a good one," says Blip. "We want a photograph of the Indians that whipped the Seventh Cavalry!"

Fort Sill's wagon master ties up the team and one by one the Cavalrymen jump out. Centerfielder Private Tom T. Benteen, followed by left fielder Lieutenant Hugh L. Scott, second baseman Sergeant Ned Hickcock, right fielder Private Philip Kearney, catcher Sergeant Jack Sullivan, third baseman Lieutenant William Cooper, first baseman Sergeant Autie Leon Reed, shortstop Sergeant Major Andy Smith, pitcher Private Jack Stout, and relief pitcher Lieutenant Colonel Paddy McKnight. The other soldiers from Fort Sill push their way through the crowd to take the bench on the third base side.

The baseball players on both teams know each other, and remain friendly despite the newspaper's public relations buildup. The last cavalryman out of the wagon is the team's batboy, an Indian kid around eleven or twelve who's dressed up like Thornton. It's clear he's proud to be dressed like a real Seventh Cavalry soldier.

Hope looks over at Nita Goingsnake to see if she's watching the batboy from Fort Sill strut his way to the visitor's dugout. Thankfully she's ignoring him. Nita is Albert's thirteen-year-old daughter and Miko Kings' batboy. For the past two seasons she's kept the knobs in order during the games. She often has a keen eye for selecting the right bat for each player. This past season, when Henri visited the Hillerich and Bradsby bat factory in Kentucky, he took Albert and Nita along to help select the best billets for the team's special order. When the fifty Louisville Sluggers arrived, Nita was the one who culled two of the maple bats that had minor defects in them and shipped them back to the factory.

The Seventh Cavalrymen's batboy has long braids. He smiles and waves at the crowd. Then he waves at the Miko Kings players in the dugout.

The Indians wave back.

"Looks like their batboy is right proud of his uniform," says Goingsnake.

"Maybe we need to get Nita a Miko Kings uniform," says Lucius.

Goingsnake spits. "Ask her. I bet she'd rather drop dead than dress like Old Man Goingsnake."

Lucius hollers to Nita, who's arranging the bats. "See that kid over there? You want to wear one of our uniforms?"

Nita doesn't reply but picks up a bat and knocks a ball toward Lucius' head.

"That's my girl!" shouts Albert.

Lucius laughs. "Okay." Then he turns to Hope. "You know who the kid is, or what tribe he's from?"

Hope shakes his head. "Judging from the braids, I'd say he's Comanche. But Comanches usually don't grin that much."

"Reckon they got him drunk?"

"Doubt it," says Blip, spitting tobacco. "But maybe he's one of them Choctaw Chucklers from Mississippi—like a certain feller I know."

"That ain't funny, Blip," says Lucius.

"Yes it is," laughs Hope.

Lucius then pulls a lady's hatpin out of his shirt. "Got this all sharpened up—just in case of a tie."

Blip gives Lucius a stern look. "Put that away! No stabbing runners on first."

Albert and Lucius exchange looks and laugh. "Tell you what," says Albert, changing the subject. "I heard the Frisco made seven trips between Roff and Ada carrying passengers coming to the game."

Another blast from a steam whistle, followed by two short blasts, can be heard in the distance. Conversation ceases until the train passes.

"That's the Katy, loaded up and heading out of town. Last one 'til midnight," says Nolan Berryhill.

"Listen, there's gonna be plenty of sore losers tonight. Let's make sure it's the gamblers and not us," says Blip, pulling notes out of his back pocket. "Napoleon, you're first batter up. Watch out for Stout's spitball. Lately you've been chopping at the ball. Stout will try and trick you again on his first pitch. Don't let him. Lucius, this guy's gonna pound you with every pitch. Watch for a change-up on three. Base hit, Lucius. That's what we want from you. Nolan…"

Hope steps out of the dugout to search for Justina. By now the ballpark is jammed. Indians from all over the territory are standing along both sides of the foul lines. In the distance, he sees Goingsnake's two little boys tossing dollar-deads in the outfield. Nolan's little girl is batting a ball to Isom Joel's daughter, who is playing catcher. He likes watching his teammate's children playing ball. He and Justina want children. Where can she be? He scans the crowd more carefully.

Surely she's gotten over the uproar he had with her cousin, Bo Hash. Hope chides himself. He should have pounded Bo's head in for asking him to throw the last game, but he didn't. He owes him for saving Justina's life seven years ago. If it hadn't been for Bo, she might have died in jail. For that he's eternally grateful. Still, Hash managed to wiggle in and get his picture taken with the rest of the team, so he can't be too upset at Hope. Just goes to show that you can't insult a chiseler.

Hope finally sees Justina and Ezol sitting side by side in the fourth row. Their heads are together, looking at a piece of cloth. He smiles. Ever since he found out that Ezol had been at Good Land when his baby sister Helema had died, he's had a soft spot in his heart for her.

Just then, the announcer calls Henri Day and Major General Shelby Thornton to the pitcher's mound, and Hope takes his place in the dugout. "Folks, let's give Henri Day and Shelby Thornton a big hand. Both men deserve applause for the great ball clubs we see here today," shouts Doc Suggs through a bullhorn.

Doc Suggs beckons a group of men carrying guitars, wearing red cowboy shirts with black fringe and white cowboy hats, onto the baseball diamond. "We're gonna have a little opening entertainment. Please welcome the Indian Territory Singers. They'll entertain us with a little song—one, I wager, you all know. Ladies and gentlemen please, sing along."

*After the bases are gone*
*After we've all come home*
*Nothing but red dirt in my skivvies*
*My back and ribs is sore*
*May I never go back*
*for another crack at the bat, Honey*
*Until the bases are loaded once more.*

The crowd applauds.

"One more time," says Suggs.

*After the bases are gone*
*After we've all come home*
*Nothing but red dirt in my skivvies*
*My back and ribs is sore…*

Then Hope hears someone yell, "Play ball!" But that other damn song repeats instead.

*Because the world is round, it turns me on*
*Because the world is round, Ah*
*Because the wind is high, it blows my mind*


"Hey, No Hands, time to take your shot. Wake up. You playing ball again, man? That game ended sixty years ago."

"What?" he asks, realizing he's holding up arms that have no hands. He examines them; they resemble two giant sea horses with curled fleshy ends for tails, instead of hands. He puts them down and they seem to float in sheets of clouds, instead of under the sea where they belong.

"Shouldn't these be in water?" he says weakly.

"Oh man, you're flying. It's the morphine. It's for the pain, remember?"

He doesn't remember.

"How many fingers am I holding up?" asks the nurse.

"Dusky Long-Gone Girl. Is that you?"

"You're stoned, No Hands. It's 1969. Remember? We just talked about the Beatles releasing *Abbey Road?* It's going platinum? And civil unrest is everywhere in America? Hell, even the Indians in Ada are going to protest against the Vietnam War."

He closes his eyes and hears his nurse crooning along with the music on the loudspeaker. *"Because the wind is high..."*

"Hey, No Hands!" snaps the voice. "Don't go back to sleep on me, old man. C'mon, we've been through this before. Who am I? Say my name!"

"John Lennon, my-nurse-not-the-singer," he says, opening his eyes.

"Good. Stay with me, man. Don't go back to sleep. You and I, we're together on the warpath. Right?"

"Right," he answers.

"We're fighting diabetes *and* John Wayne movies, right?"

"Right."

"Wanna take your insulin shot?"

"Why not? But first tell me what happened to these," he asks, raising up the sea horses.

"Diabetes, I imagine," says John. "But maybe it was that woman you're always talking about. Maybe she cut them off in a fit of rage. Then there's the story you told me of how you and some gambler were in cahoots, and got caught making bets against your own team. He was murdered and you lost your hands. You've told so many stories. How would I know the truth?"

Hope blinks a few times, coming into consciousness as his nurse gently shoves a needle in his belly. He doesn't feel a thing. "Say, did I ever ask you if you played baseball?"

"About a million times."

"Well, do you?"

"Yep. I'm the catcher for a fast-pitch softball team. Sometimes we play out at Kullihoma, the Chickasaw Nation's land out east of town. You know Kullihoma?" asks John.

"Sure do," says Hope, rubbing his face with a mangled forearm. "We used to play out there some sixty years ago. The field is down in the sandy bottoms."

"That's the place," says his nurse.

At that moment, a loud scream reverberates down the hall of the nursing home. It's high pitched, as if someone has seen a ghost. John goes to investigate and quickly returns, dragging an apparition into Hope's room.

"Ouch, you're hurting me!" says the tall bulky Indian wearing a red-and-white polka-dot dress and a bright orange wig.

"Take that off!" commands John. "Take that off right this minute."

"John, for God's sake, please stop yelling. I just thought it was a good time to protest for personal change, while we're protesting against the Vietnam War. Power to the people, man," says the apparition.

"Take that dress off before I pole-ax you!"

"Don't you dare hit me, you Comanche brute!"

Hope tries to interrupt. "John, take it easy. It's only Kerwin."

"Oh, you recognize this fairy, but me, a Comanche warrior from the great Comanche Nation, you mistake for a woman you knew fifty years ago? Morphine fog my ass," says John.

"No, it's just *chim lakchi,* John. It's nothing," he says, looking around the room for his hands. He tries to remember where they are. How they came to be lost. Once, his fingers could speak a whole language. They gestured to Goingsnake like the earth calls rain. The two never missed a single message on the ballfield—except for that one time...but that was his mistake, not Goingsnake's. How he misses Albert. And his hands and fingers. The real mystery of pitching is in the fingers. He must have pitched 25,000 fastballs before his arm, wrist, and fingers could properly reverse the ball. But where are they now? He must find them. Hope feels the room move. Only pale reflections of his two nurses remain. The tiny candle flame wavers, as if kissed by a gentle breeze. It throws dim shadows across their faces, or so it seems. He turns his head to face the darkness. Inside *yakni kula,* where they put him, ghosts meander unperturbed. And by some strange coincidence, he can see the world as it really is.

The year is 1896. Hope knows this because the school's principal, the Reverend Clark, repeatedly tells time for the students. He says that in the coming twentieth century, four years hence, there will be no more wild Indians. Education will see to that.

The place where they put him is a solitary cell underground. The only light comes from a punk candle on the floor next to a bit of damp straw. To ventilate it, the school's janitor drilled holes through the wooden plank that holds up the dirt roof. Hope Little Leader falls asleep curled up on a small cot and dreams of a different future for himself than the one they say he is destined for. Something frightens him awake. He shivers. Wincing in the darkness, he recalls the harangue he received in front of the entire student body.

"Mr. Little Leader, how many times have you tried to run away from this school?"

"Twelve times, sir."

"How old are you?"

"Fourteen, sir."

"What do you want to be when you grow up?"

"A baseball player, like my uncle Ahojebo Little Leader, sir."

"It is with regret that we must visit punishment upon you, son," says the Reverend Clark. "But it is equally humiliating to the other Indian students, and to their tribes, that you continue to run down the streets of Hampton like some wild animal sprung from a trap. Warriors of manly bearing, even future baseball players, do not run away. You must learn self-discipline and to follow orders."

Hope watches the reverend.

"Do you understand why you are being punished?"

"Yes, sir. I run."

"For this reason, you will be placed in solitary confinement so you may contemplate your future. You are relieved from the boy's baseball team and you will remain locked up until I deem you fit to come out among the other students. You will be allowed out only to attend your classes. Is this understood?"

Hope stares miserably at his captor. A hush comes over the other students. Finally he looks around the room, shrugs his shoulders, and replies in Choctaw, his voice not angry, but stern.

"I am a man and I am strong. You are stupid and pitiful. Now, at last, I will get some sleep." Then he spits on the floor for emphasis, which ends up costing him even more time.

Hope doesn't want to relive his humiliation in front of the other students, but he can't help himself. He gets up from the cot and stands in the darkness. There is no motion of air, no shadows. He feels around for the punk candle, left over from a fellow student. He lights it and the flame illuminates his memory. He doesn't understand all the English, but knows the gist of what is happening.

The Indians call Hampton "The Reservation," because there are so many different tribes represented. Every waking moment is organized for them. The teachers discourage personal beliefs, rituals, and traditions. His head swims with different names, and he can no longer distinguish the different white faces. Everyone is strange, not like his Choctaw relatives at home. The Indian students are trapped here. Like chameleons in a basket, the trick is to become invisible, blend in, and stay out of trouble. He understands now why blending in is important. A few weeks ago, when he took his plate outside and offered corn to *Hashtali,* the eye of the sun, the one who watches over all Choctaws, a teacher scolded him for wasting food. Frowning with annoyance and shielding her face from *Hashtali's* rays, the white woman motioned for one of the older students to bring him to her.

"These ideas of yours are the work of the devil, young man. Please put the food back on your plate," she said in hushed tones. "Take the plate to the cook. We do not waste food here."

"I pray and hoe garden every day!" he shouted.

Hope threw the plate of food across the yard and sat on the ground.

It felt warm and clay hard. His heart pounded and sweat rolled down his back. It was as if *Hashtali* had detonated above him and he burned in the flames that roared, shrieked, and consumed his body.

He has to find a way back home. He'll run away or die trying.

Confined for now, Hope stares into the candle flame and tries to remember all that he has learned at the school. Never feed the spirits in front of white people. They punish you for that. Keep your thoughts to yourself.

Hope begins to sing a warrior's song, calling on the spirits for help.

*We hi ya We hi ya ha yuyu yuyu ha!*
*We hi ya ha We he ya ha yuyu yuyu ha!*

Then, suddenly, he catches a memory of the principal's words floating out of the fecal dust inside the cell. "It is here where Indians like you must come and learn the habits of good industry. You will learn in time, Mr. Little Leader, that confinement is sometimes necessary, even among *family*." When the principal emphasized the word *family* he pulled his face into a pleasant disguise. "You see," he added, "by cultivating you wild Indians…we tame the land."

Hope can still remember how the Reverend looked that day as he walked past him, singing a song.

*Amazing Grace, how sweet the sound,*
*That saved a wretch like me.*

Hope knows why he was placed at Hampton Normal School for Blacks and Indians. A preacher named Clyde Spencer came around to his mother's place and told her there had never been any Choctaws at Hampton. He said her son and two daughters would be good role models at the school because Choctaws were known for their fine dispositions. When the minister found out that Ahojebo Little Leader was Hope's uncle, he hinted that the boy could play on Hampton's baseball team.

Hope's mother said "go away, man" many times. However, not long after Mr. Spencer's visit, his mother's body began to waste away. Hope wondered if the minister was a *Nan isht ahollo*. Maybe that witch put bad medicine on his mother's back when she wasn't looking. He'd been told that *Nan isht ahollo* could cause death merely by touching their victims. Yes, he thought, the witch killed his mother. He was sure of it now. Her skin became so transparent that even the delicate veins on her collarbone were visible. On the night she died, his mother peered at him with large eyes that seemed to dangle out of her face. "I'm going, son. Look after my girls."

At that moment the whole cabin became luminous, although only embers smoldered in the fireplace. Outside, the wind suddenly howled violently, as if a tornado was coming. The small house shook and rattled. All through the storm he and his sisters maintained a vigil next to their mother's body. Hope believed the wind itself was in mourning with them. At daybreak, his grandfather dug the grave. Because his mother had been propped up before she died, her mouth had hung open for almost a day before they wrapped her in her favorite blue-and-green quilt and placed her in the ground. Hope's grandfather tried to close her jaw, but it wouldn't shut. Just before they lowered her in the ground, the quilt slipped from around his mother's face. Somehow his mother had closed her mouth. She looked refreshed and peaceful when they began to cover her with the red dirt of their land.

Two months later, Hope and his sisters ended up boarding the train to Virginia with the *Nan isht ahollo* and his wife, Mrs. Spencer. At the depot, his grandfather, speaking in Choctaw, assured him that his uncle Ahojebo would come after them. "As soon as he finds out you've been taken, he'll come for you. He's young enough to be appointed your guardian. Not like this old one," said his grandfather, pointing to himself. The old man added, "When you and your sisters return, we'll eat pumpkin soup." Then he pressed a snake rattle into Hope's hands and draped a quilt around the two little girls. "Don't let them steal any loose hairs from your head."

As the train pulled out of the depot, Hope leaned out the window to look for his grandfather. In the distance he saw the old man running headlong into the arms of a raging tornado. Hope rubbed his eyes. He wouldn't understand the vision until many years later.

Mrs. Spencer pulled Hope away from the window and seated him next to Lucinda and Helema, his two sisters. The three of them remained together until they reached Hampton, Virginia.

Shortly after they arrived, Hope was told that he and his sisters couldn't stay. The school didn't want Indians from the Five Civilized Tribes because they'd once held slaves, and because the Choctaws had their own schools in Indian Territory. It was a mistake that they had been brought there. The news made Hope very happy. But without telling Hope, the principal decided at the last minute to keep him, while sending his sisters on to Good Land, an orphanage for Indians near Doaksville, in Indian Territory. When the wagon carrying his two sisters pulled out of Hampton's schoolyard, Hope, who had been working in the garden, saw them and ran after the wagon.

*"Falamat ia. Katimma ish-ia?* Come back! Where are you going?"

Helema, his baby sister, stretched her arms toward him and tried to jump from the wagon, but Mrs. Spencer held her back. His eight-year-old sister Lucinda yelled *"Hopai-a-a-a-,"* releasing the *a* as she ran out of breath.

He ran as fast as he could across the schoolyard. The school's janitor, George Lincoln, a full-grown black man, tackled him before he could reach the wagon. He held Hope on the ground until his screaming sisters were out of sight.

"Mr. Lincoln, let up me!" he shouted, trying to put his English words together. *"Aichna!"* Unexpectedly he began to shake all over, his mouth open, but no more words would come out.

The janitor held him down but whispered into his ear, "It don't do no good to die here. White folks'll jest parade your body around town asking for more donations. I know how you feel, boy." George Lincoln picked him up and rocked him like a baby. "I know how you feel." Then he carried Hope to *yakni kula* so he could not run after his sisters.


Two weeks have passed since Lucinda and Helema were driven away. Hope prays for his lost sisters. He prays to the spirit of his mother to help them. Alone at night, he hears insects crawling in and out of the walls. If he closes his eyes, he can pretend he is hunting blue frogs at his mother's pond. Now that he's safe in *yakni kula* he prays to *Hashtali* by using the candle flame. He tells *Miko Luak,* fire, how he came to be lost at the school. Every morning they let him out to attend classes in reading, writing, and arithmetic. He has trouble pronouncing the r's. But in arithmetic, he gets to be with his true love, Dusky Long-Gone Girl. Then, back in isolation, he has time to think about her. Does she love him too? He wants to marry her someday. Their oldest son will become a pitcher. They will call him Ahojebo, after his uncle.

Hope surveys his pitiful state. General Armstrong must have started Hampton to punish Indians. Soldiers hate Indians. Everyone knows that. Just then, bad air snakes down through the holes and licks at the candle flame. A voice shouts down into *yakni kula,* "God loves you." Then recoils. *Nan isht ahollo* must be everywhere, he thinks.

For a long while, Hope Little Leader holds on to the silence, trapped on the underside of the world. He pushes against the dugout door, then pounds it with his fists as hard as he can. "*Chim lakchi.* I will get out of here, I will play ball like my uncle, and I will marry Dusky Long-Gone Girl."

"*Chim lakchi.* This is nothing."


"Nothing?" says Kerwin Johnston. "What are you talking about? I'm freedom marching in a dress, not some U.S. army uniform."

"Sorry, Kerwin," says Hope, blinking at his two night nurses. "I was back in the dugout, but I'm keeping up with current events."

Hope raises his head and inspects the dress his male nurse is wearing. "Can't say as you look free to me, but you might pass for *Ohoyo Holba.*"

"*Ohoyo Holba,*" says Kerwin, contemplating the Choctaw words. "What does that mean?"

"Like a woman, but not," says Hope.

Kerwin pulls the orange wig off, tosses it onto Hope's bed.

Then he leans in close and whispers, "You still reliving those days when you had hands?"

Hope winks. "I'm going to put my hat on Dusky Long-Gone Girl's bed. If she leaves it there, that means she wants me as her husband."

John Lennon ignores Hope's last remark and continues shouting at Kerwin. "What the hell is wrong with you, man? Dressing up like that! Protest march or not! You're scaring these poor elders to death."

Hope knows it's his responsibility as the elder in the room to stop the young men from arguing, but he's tired and his hands are ice cold. They ache something terrible. He closes his eyes and, as usual, his mind begins to wander.

A successful run, he will learn in the coming years, is when an Indian slides into home plate. When Hope opens his eyes, the nurses are gone. However, the spider is quietly spinning her silk threads into a baseball diamond in the corner of the dugout. By candlelight he can see her mourning the death of her lover. First, she peels back his head from his body, then cherishes his hands as food.

# 4
## The Martyr of Hope
### New Orleans, Louisiana, June 1969

"People need stories. Our beliefs, our cultural heroes and heroines, are created in stories. It is through stories that people transcend time and enter into the world of immortality. But what becomes of living legends, heroes and heroines who've been frozen in time and isolated from their communities as they were lifted to eminence? Even the greatest champions are mistaken for people they never were. And as the years pass, historians have them speaking words they never said.

"So how does an ordinary woman become a heroine, even a legend, among blacks in Old New Orleans? After such an early public, activist life, why did she retreat to live anonymously among common citizens? These are but a few of the questions that I, Algernon Pinchot, Assistant Professor at Morehouse College, will try to answer in the biography I am researching on Justina Maurepas, also known as 'Black Juice.' My book, entitled *Black Juice, the Martyr of Hope,* will highlight the life of a woman important to Black Nationalists.

"Madame Maurepas' life is associated with two early twentieth century events for Black Nationalists. The first is the New Orleans race riots on Wednesday, July 25, 1900, when whites massacred black cooks, busboys, prostitutes, shoeshine boys, piano players, and barbers after Robert Charles, a black man, shot seven white police officers. The violence was halted that evening by a dynamite explosion in the Storyville District. Black Juice was jailed and charged with anarchism, but later released on grounds of insufficient evidence.

"The second incident is the day Dr. Marcus Garvey was deported, December 2, 1927, when another mysterious detonation went off at the docks in the port of New Orleans—suspected again to be the work of Black Juice and her followers. But that allegation was never proved.

"Exiled from New Orleans in November 1900 and told never to return, Black Juice is rumored to have come back to Louisiana in the fall of 1907, this time to the swamps to teach in a one-room school-house for Houma Indians.

"She is absent again from history until 1923, when federal court records proclaim her the lover of William Shakespeare, the Negro 'Chief of Police' of the United Negro Improvement Association, a Marcus Garvey project. Both Shakespeare and his accomplice, Fred Dyer, were accused of murdering J.W.H. Eason, a black minister who was to testify against Garvey in the Black Star Line mail fraud case. In 1939, at age sixty-one, she re-emerges from the shadows of history as the third wife of a New Orleans shipping magnate, the Frenchman Gerard Louis Maurepas, age seventy-five. A white man. Two months after their marriage he dies, leaving her a substantial fortune. To say her life has been filled with contradictions is obvious but insufficient."

I push the stop button on my tape recorder. On my first meeting with the Great Lady, it will be too off-putting to lug the recorder into her home. I will have to rely on my notes and my wits—if she agrees to speak candidly with me. Three times this week I have driven to her home to attempt to arrange an interview, and three times I have been turned away. First by her lawyer, then her doctor, and finally by her devoted housekeeper. Her great-granddaughter, however, took pity on me and by telephone has assured me of a one-hour interview.

So once again I drive to the home of Black Juice, on Magazine Street in Uptown. The Spanish governor Esteban Rodriguez Miro y Sabater is said to have built *"Magazin,"* the warehouse, for trade goods awaiting export in the late eighteenth century. I suppose *Magazin* suits the legacy of Black Juice, as she herself is a mixture of old and new world genealogy. How long she has lived at her current residence remains a mystery.

Few these days gain admittance to her formal salon, which I am told has a dark atmosphere of blood reds, blackberry blues, and muddy greens—colors suggestive of an ominous past. Then there are the rumors of her collection of mysterious American Indian relics.

As I straighten my tie, brush the fuzz from my blue blazer, I note the sweat in the creases of my palms and on my brow. I use a handkerchief to wipe away my hot anticipation. When the door finally opens, the same housekeeper who formerly turned me away now escorts me down a long corridor and onto the veranda.

Although it is a stifling August morning, Black Juice wears a long-sleeved white cotton dress. She is seated on a veranda off the first floor of the house and, as one might expect, is tiny and frail, aged, but otherwise seems in good health. The pupil of her left eye is cloudy, perhaps obstructed by a cataract. Around her neck is a gold chain and crucifix. Her skin is more red than black and I can see that she also has freckles. I account for this from her family background, a mixture of Louisiana Indian, African, and French. Her thinning hair is very long, speckled black and white, mostly white, like the tail feathers of some exotic Caribbean bird. Quite remarkable, I think, for a woman of ninety one.

I begin with all of the courtesies that come with French culture in New Orleans. Then, I position my notepad on my lap and, with her permission, I start our session with a simple question. I ask if she has knowledge of the songs written about her.

Black Juice says she does not read or write in English. I do not believe her, as her history suggests otherwise. But French is the only language in which she will converse.

"English was not the first language in my home, nor at the school at Sacred Heart. My first language was French, then came Latin. I have said that I heard the songs written for me, songs I don't deserve. I was the one who chose to bear the weight of death. That is all."

"You are speaking of the dynamite you carried?" I ask, in English.

Silence.

I address her again in French, asking about her life in Storyville, hoping this will win her confidence, and show that I have read the accounts of the many brothels and their clients, detailed in a New Orleans scandal sheet, *The Mascot*.

Black Juice remains silent. She looks down and covers her face with her right hand, attempting to hide her sorrow. Finally she looks up. "Monsieur Pinchot, you keep asking about my past. I keep it closed in here," she says, pointing to her heart.

This time her eyes fill with tears that spill over her bold cheekbones. I quickly try to change the mood. "Do you ever listen to the songs that Eubie Blake wrote for you? You are the heroine in one of his musicals."

"I told you English is a language I do not..."

"May I sing some of the lines in French?"

"If you like, but..."

> *Black Juice*
> *Black Juice*
> *The beautiful and the terrible*
> *Martyr of hope*
> *Bring us your potion*
> *Teach us a notion*
> *Or two,*
> *We'll blow the white house down in slow motion*
> *Black Juice*
> *Black Juice*
> *The beautiful and the terrible*
> *Martyr of hope.*

I stop because I can see that I am annoying her.

"It wasn't like that, you see," she replies in French. "The words have created the legend. Nothing more. Black Juice of the songs is one thing. Madame Justina Maurepas, the woman, the lover of hope—the word, I mean—she is someone else."

"Not a champion of Black Nationalism," I say.

"I am afraid not," she answers, wiping her eyes with a delicate lace handkerchief. "But I can't help but smile when I think about the legendary figure you call Black Juice. Who is she? Where does she live? Does she still contemplate our struggle for justice? Yes. For civil rights? Yes. Does she repudiate the racial hatred that rose up last year and murdered the only black American to win a Nobel Peace Prize? Yes. Does she regularly consider that black men are dying every day in that ridiculous slaughterhouse called Vietnam? Yes, Monsieur, yes!"

Black Juice leans forward in her chair, and her hand is now drawn into a clenched fist. At last I see the essence of the legend coming to life before me. "But my friend," she says forcefully, "I failed long ago in my struggles against violence and inequality. In fact, you could say I succumbed to it. With what little time I have left, I choose to ponder my mother's life. Her life is far more interesting to me now. My poor father, and even my great-great-grandmother Maria Humming Bird, who once lived in Santo Domingo in Haiti at the foot of the mountains, near the port of Cape Francois—their lives were much more revolutionary than mine. Did you know my grandmother's village was called Pocito Haitien? Little Haiti. No one in New Orleans has ever heard of it. It is the same with Black Juice. No one in 1969 knows of her outside the little ditties the children sing. The public believes she is dead and that is as it should be, do you not agree?"

Black Juice settles back in her chair. For a long moment she studies my face. "Monsieur Pinchot, I am told you are a historian."

"Yes, that is correct. My research concerns the birth of Black Nationalism."

"Then why are you interested in Black Juice? What greatness did she achieve? Although we were together for only a short while, hope and me, nothing would ever come of it. I am of course speaking of the desire to be equal. You see…"

The Great Lady takes the handkerchief and wipes her mouth and eyes before continuing.

"I foolishly believed, as others did, that we should destroy what we could not change…" She pauses and fingers her cross, and doesn't complete her thought. She tilts her head to the left as if listening to hushed voices. A ghost memory has walked onto the veranda and I am now the intruder from Morehouse interrupting her solitude and whatever peace she has made with herself. At last she returns to the present, and I realize she's not living in the past, but contemplating her future. Death. Finally she speaks.

"Monsieur."

"Yes, Madame."

"Hope was mercy. Do you understand?"

"No, Madame, but I can try if you will let me."

Black Juice bows her head and for the first time I notice the mark of a deep scar along her hairline. "Hope was mercy in my mouth," she says softly.

"But if you once had hope, how did you move from white dresses and the French sisters of the Sacred Heart to explosions and brutality?"

"Like all journeys, Monsieur, it was fated," she says slowly. "As a historian, you must know that it is important to consider the early period of Louisiana and its effects on the original parishes. So when I talk of my family as intellectuals, as wealthy people, and say that I never knew the lingering hardships of slavery, I'm really talking about a period of time long before I was born. When I was a small child, all the French people I knew in my parish were like me. A mixture of many things. I guess you could say that I was the one who was colorblind—and that is certainly true of my choices in men."

She begins to laugh. "You know, I told my great-granddaughter that under no circumstances would I discuss my past with you and yet I am doing it."

I sense that she's warming up to me, so I press on. "But Madame, how can we know the truth of your story if you will not speak it? You accuse historians like me of inventing your life. Only you can tell it. There are generations of blacks who have not experienced your reality, but they know inequality and prejudice. And we live in a country whose hunger craves the blood of great black men such as Martin Luther King!"

Black Juice seems amused by my passionate outburst. "I knew his grandfather," she says, smiling ever so slightly. "I met the elder Mr. King in 1922, or perhaps it was '23. I'd gone to Atlanta to hear Marcus Garvey speak. I can't remember precise dates any longer, but we met and even exchanged a few letters."

"Madame," I say pointedly, "I know you are aware of the present, so what I propose is that these two realities, your past and the present, have a conversation."

She nods thoughtfully. Finally she says, "I can try to explain how it was for me."

"I was born Justina Lemoine in 1878, in Avoyelles Parish in Louisiana. When I was very small, maybe five or six, I wanted to become an artist. Think of that, an artist. What a thing for a colored child. At the time my mother's brothers were continually being questioned by white men. I didn't understand why, though. I only knew that my mother was always frightened. And she would weep and say how afraid she was that my uncles were going to be hanged. As you know, white Southerners hated the Fifteenth Amendment because it prevented a state from denying the vote to any person because of their race. My uncles were in constant danger. They were determined that blacks in Louisiana would be able to vote. But I didn't understand any of this. Or why my poor father, a seemingly passive Frenchman, was so different from my uncles."

Black Juice pauses. "Maybe that's why I wanted to become a painter, so that I could create happy pictures of my mother. I wanted to brush joy across her face.

"In 1892 my father sent me to Hampton Normal School for Blacks and Indians. I was fourteen. Father thought that because it was a bi-racial school, I would be treated well and could become a school-teacher. While I was at Hampton, my mother died of malaria. By that time I had come to know there was something besides being French— which I had so long been. There were terrible costs in those days to being Negro or Indian. Or both. My eldest uncle was shot. Mother's youngest brother was beaten to death. He was only nineteen, and yet every major bone in his body was broken. But I think it was when Mother died that…"

She breaks down. I realize that the fighter of the legend, the twenty-two year old who, on July 25, 1900, purportedly took three sticks of dynamite and headed down to the red-light district to blow it up, is ailing. Not just from her advanced age, but from something more lethal: her unspoken sorrow. The night of July 25, 1900, is steeped in

New Orleans folklore. Buddy Bolden, the father of jazz, was playing his cornet on a bandstand near Franklin and the old Custom House Street. When the white mob came screaming down the streets his band had to run for cover. Buddy Bolden purportedly lost his waistcoat and watch—and maybe his flight from the mob hastened his own mental breakdown.

But the legend of Black Juice was born on that night, when she allegedly walked into the Courtesan, one of the more famous brothels in the Storyville District, and lit the dynamite. An iceman, who claimed to know her, said he saw her running from the Courtesan. Seconds later, the building was a mishmash of bricks, broken glass, and dead bodies. Three other brothels were dynamited that night, so she wasn't alone in her efforts. When she was finally caught and taken to jail, she was interrogated for seven days without food or water. Later it was hinted in the newspaper that she'd been passed around among the jailers, but still she would not betray her cohorts.

By now Black Juice has dried her eyes. "There were many just like me. Day laborers from the docks. Nursemaids, livery boys. All of us in our own way were fighting for equality. For those of us who are still alive—we are like black crows, lazily circling death. We're not in a hurry to depart, but depart soon we must."

"Hopefully, Madame, you will not depart without telling your story," I say. "Did you work at the Courtesan?"

"I did. But as a teacher, not a prostitute. You realize, Monsieur Pinchot, that from 1897 until 1917, prostitution was legal in the Storyville District." She leans back against her chair. "Even the children of prostitutes need to learn to read and write," she says softly.

"The court record says that you were accused of being part of an underground organization that was teaching blacks that they were equal to whites."

"I was also teaching arithmetic."

"Then why destroy the only home these children had?"

Black Juice is silent. She bows her head. Her eyes are fixed on a small square of lace she holds in her hand. I fear I have so offended her that at any moment I may be asked to leave.

"Monsieur, have you ever held a small boy in your arms after he has been so thoroughly sodomized that he dies of exhaustion—and loss of blood?"

I clear my throat. "No Madame," I say softly. "I am ashamed to say I have not considered that such things could have happened."

Her eyes narrow as she continues speaking. "There were many such cases. Just who do you suppose was reporting those atrocities to *The Mascot?*"

"Forgive me," I say. "I should have guessed it would be you."

"There were many in our group who were trying to expose what was happening. At that time there were no societies against the cruelty of children. A few days before the Charles shootings, one of our members had stolen a box of dynamite. As soon as the riots began, we quickly put it to use. We thought we could shut down Storyville."

I probe her memory with other details I have found in the newspaper archives. "A local priest wrote a letter to the editor of the *Southern Republican* claiming that the police tortured you. He says they put hot coals on your body. When Mr. DuBois recounted these events in his magazine *The Crisis* some nine years later, he gave you credit for focusing attention on the child sex market—for the most part Black and Indian children—in the district."

Silence.

"I have also read that Orleans Parish never had an eyewitness against you. There was no iceman."

"What possible difference could it make now?" she says.

"Is that true?" I ask.

She nods slowly. "Yes, but it changes nothing. People were killed. Buildings were ruined. Eventually life was restored as it was before. Only the scars we carry remain. That's the problem when rage is unleashed. Nothing is solved. We thought we could bring liberation from suffering, but in truth we only brought destruction."

We sit in silence for a moment until I bring up another delicate subject. "I read in one of the accounts that a flimflam man named

Beauregard Hash bribed a judge for your release."

Black Juice smiles a little. "Beauregard was my second cousin. He's long dead."

"Excuse me. I didn't realize he was a relation, or I would have phrased it more delicately."

"Beauregard was what he was. He came to a sorry end on his own. I guess you could say we were a matched pair. Ill-fated, I mean. But Beauregard came to my rescue in New Orleans because my mother and his mother were cousins, and for that I am eternally grateful."

"Mr. Hash was quoted in the *Southern Republican* stating that you were 'nearly kilt' in prison?"

"And how do you find me today?"

"You are well, Madame."

"Barely alive, I should think. But I would not be here now if it weren't for my great-granddaughter, who plagues me day and night, who will not leave me for a moment, nor go off to college, until she's satisfied that I will live on forever."

"Is she aware of your past in Indian Territory?"

"Some of it."

"Does she want to mimic your radical choices?"

"She is too intelligent for that."

"I suppose we do not want to give up on the legend of Black Juice," I say.

"Monsieur, please forget her. There are more important stories in America. Life is what it is. And, remember, there will always be people to fight injustice, some with more mercy than perhaps I."

A late-afternoon shower cools things off a bit. From the veranda, we watch a yard crow jump a small lizard as it runs across the steps of the Maurepas house. As I prepare to leave, Evangeline, her great-granddaughter, brings a vase full of white gardenias and places them on the white wicker table. She hands one to Black Juice.

"These are Grandmama's favorite flowers," she says to me in English. "I think it's because they remind her of her greatest love, a famous baseball player." She turns and whispers, conspiratorially, "He was a wild Indian."

The Great Lady frowns. *"Hush!"* she says in English.

"So, Madame, you do speak the language of English queens!" She smiles sheepishly at me, then at her great-granddaughter.

"Evangeline is lovely," she says. "No?"

*"Oui, Madame. Mon seul regret est d'en avoir à peine vu la couleur."*

Evangeline laughs and says, "But you must return, and plan to stay longer. If not for Grandmama's stories, then to see me. Did you know that I'm named for her daughter, my grandmother?" she asks. "There's another mystery you must uncover—Grandmama's racy life among the Indians."

*"Vous m'avez fait découvrir un monde entièrement nouveau,"* I say.

They both laugh. But I can see clearly how the Great Lady dotes on the girl. Evangeline can't be much over eighteen. Her long brown hair is very straight, and she appears as exotic as her grandmama.

Black Juice studies us both. "What I cannot understand," she says, looking directly at Evangeline, "is why are you are telling these things to a man you have just met. Is it because Professor Pinchot is single, very handsome, and black?"

I blush. *"Madame, parlons-en tout en prenant un café,"* I say, trying to hold on to my dignity as a scholar. I can see that Evangeline is enjoying my predicament. She smiles, but says nothing.

As I prepare to leave, Black Juice asks Evangeline to fetch a wheelchair and her glasses. It's then I discover that the Great Lady has a prosthetic leg. I didn't know of her situation. This may explain why she has not been seen in public for many years. When did this happen, I wonder. I offer my assistance helping her into the wheelchair. Considering her age, I am amazed at the strength the frail-looking woman still possesses.

"Monsieur Pinchot," she says, slightly out of breath. "I have decided to invite you to return tomorrow. Evangeline seems to want you here."

Black Juice wipes the lens of her glasses and puts them on. She leans forward and looks at me. "I once had a friend," she says, "a young Choctaw woman named Ezol, who claimed that tree branches grew over her eyes. Now at my advanced age, I have cataracts and know just how she felt. Come closer. I want to look you over."

I take off my blue blazer and wish I had not perspired so during our first meeting. At last she smiles at me. "If you come back, I will convey a different story than the one you heard today. I may be the only one who can tell it. Even if at times I am a bit muddled, I remember my life in Indian Territory more clearly than my activities just last week. Sometimes at night when I hear the cicadas singing, I think I am back in Ada. Back in my rightful place with Hope…"

She pauses and waves me away. I take a few steps back and watch as Evangeline tends to her grandmama. The two exchange words of comfort, and after another short discussion in hushed tones, the Great Lady calls me back to her side.

"Monsieur, perhaps if I tell you more of my life you will understand that I'm a heroine only of the imagination. You see," she says, "when I became involved with Mr. Shakespeare, I was still eating anger for breakfast, lunch, and dinner over all the injustices my family and I had suffered. We were a straw fire, the two of us…a flash in the pan. Then many years later, I married my late husband, Monsieur Maurepas. He was a lovely, courteous man. We connected because of our families' histories. Perhaps he reminded me of my father. But because we knew each other so little before his death, today he seems much more like a dream than a flesh and blood man."

She takes a deep breath. "I have embraced many branches of the tree. And I have many regrets, but my greatest is the loss of the one man I truly loved, Hope Little Leader. I know how strange that must sound to you today, coming from the woman you have admired as Black Juice. But my view of life has greater perspective than you can imagine at your age. Hope was beautiful and young, much like you. In 1907 he was twenty-five years old, with forearms as hard as a statue. This is the man I turned away from. Oh, there were many reasons, many justifications, but the truth is I ran away from him because I thought he was weak. What I mistook for his failings were indeed his strengths. If you come back I will not talk about the Black Juice of New Orleans, but I will tell a much more interesting account and history—of the time when I was the lover of Hope Little Leader, the father of my only daughter, Evangeline Little Leader, born in 1908 in Houma, Louisiana."

And here too is another echo of baseball's childhood memory in *Anompa Sipokni,* Old Talking Places.

They didn't have any mitts.
They didn't have baseballs.
They didn't have bats.
No uniforms, or helmets. No caps.

But they played.

# 5

## Skunks Are Sensitive

### Ada, Oklahoma, October 5, 1969

"Did I tell you about the time I witnessed one of the worst baseball collisions in Indian Territory history?" asks Hope, with his head turned away from his nurse. "Over at Krebs."

Kerwin Johnston doesn't answer. He is concentrating on gentle movements. He slides both arms beneath his patient and turns him on his side. Kerwin pushes two pillows against No Hands' back to stabilize him while he investigates a wound the day nurse had noted on the chart. What Kerwin finds is a lesion the size of a dinner plate growing across his patient's buttocks.

There is a moment of silence so profound that Kerwin can barely contain his grief. The bedsore has become infected all the way down to the bone. Once it's reached this stage it's unlikely to heal. In fact, for a man in No Hands' condition, the infection will soon become systemic and most likely cause heart failure. Kerwin blames himself. The pitiful old man wouldn't be in this shape if he'd been on the job caring for him. Kerwin knows that the day nurses don't give a shit about elderly Indians. He's overheard them say they take care of paying residents first, Indians on welfare last. Since the polka-dotted dress stunt put him on disciplinary leave without pay, the Indian patients at the nursing home have suffered. This is a hard lesson.

"We were playing the Krebs Miners on their ballfield," says No Hands, oblivious to the sad expression on Kerwin's face. "Did I tell you about it?"

"I can't remember," says Kerwin, cleaning the area around the wound.

"It was toward the end of the season, 1905. Krebs and Miko Kings were tied 2-2. A player by the name of Pete Jenkins was first baseman for Krebs. Alvin Jenkins, his brother, was catching. I hit a high foul that popped up between first base and home plate. Both brothers ran after it, their eyes on the ball. They knocked themselves smooth out. When we picked them up they were covered with blood. Pete had a broken jaw and his two front teeth were missing. His forehead was gashed and he needed about a dozen stitches. Alvin's face was cut up too. The wonder of it, though, was that Alvin had caught the ball and hung on to it," says Hope, chuckling. "And I was out."

Silence.

"Kerwin?" asks Hope.

"Yeah."

"You finished diapering my behind?"

"Not quite. Am I hurting you?"

"Nope. Don't feel a thing. Did I tell you about the first time Wild Buck Taylor put me in to pitch?"

"Tell it."

Hope coughs. "My voice is kinda raspy this morning."

"It's 5 p.m."

"Don't matter what time it is."

"Sure it does. It's dinnertime and you're gonna eat something," says Kerwin, turning Hope over on his back.

Hope rests his head on his pillow. "Whatever you say."

"Go on with your story. We'll argue later, after I've scooped some food in your mouth."

Hope laughs a little. "It was about the time Reverend Clark—you know, that principal at Hampton—decided I was just about as stubborn an Indian kid as he'd ever come across. And that's saying something because the Reverend worked with the Sioux and Cheyenne.

Or maybe his patience for handling malcontents had just run out. Whatever the case, he shipped me back to Indian Territory by way of a Choctaw agent named Bertram Bill.

"Mr. Bill said he wasn't chasing a fool kid like me all over the countryside, so he wrapped my hands and feet together and then blindfolded me. That's how I rode the train from Hampton, Virginia, all the way back to Choctaw Country, bound up like some Egyptian mummy. As soon as we got home and he found out my grandfather had died, he toted me over to Jones Academy, the school for boys near Hartshorne."

"What happened then?" asks Kerwin, absentmindedly. He flicks a syringe lightly a couple of times before injecting insulin into his patient's stomach.

"I was placed in the care of a man named Wild Buck Taylor. His way of handling ornery fellers like me was to put us all on baseball teams. Wild Buck had been a batting coach on the same Winfield Reds team as my late uncle, Ahojebo Little Leader. Once I heard that, I was devoted to Wild Buck. He told me that Ahojebo was a good man. He also was the one who explained to me how Uncle had died."

Kerwin smoothes a clean white sheet over the top of his patient and looks at Hope. "Think you can eat a little something now?"

"No thanks," says Hope. "I'm in the middle of a story."

Kerwin smiles. Every evening is the same. If the old man is clearheaded, he spins one baseball yarn after another.

"We were tied for first place against a team from Perry. Even though Perry was once part of the Choctaw district, it was pretty much an all-white school by that time. So you can imagine when the Jones Academy boys hit the ballfield, the sparks went flying. The day of the game, people from the local farms and ranches came into town in buggies and buckboards. Townspeople were sitting on the ground around all three bases. But we didn't have any supporters at the game. Just the school's wagon master, he was it. Andrew Lewis, a kid from Panola with a great arm, was on the mound for Jones. It was the bottom of the seventh. In those days kid teams didn't play more than seven innings. The eighth was for tie-breakers. Back then baseball rules in Indian Territory were different."

"You still with me?" asks Hope. "I don't see so good anymore."

"Yes," says Kerwin, as he takes Hope's pulse. "I'm with you."

"Jones was up, 3-2. There were two outs and Perry had runners on first and third. Wild Buck was a tough one, and he had one rule for the boys at Jones Academy: Whatever game we played, we should put our heart into it. The old man wasn't much of a coach either—he was kind of like a gossip. He would come out onto the field and talk to us about the other team's weaknesses and strengths. Often he'd say, 'Be mindful of what comes next. You're nine players, but you got to move with one heart on the field. Anticipate where the ball is gonna be next. See where it's gonna be before it gets there.'"

Hope coughs again. "Water."

Kerwin pours a small glass and puts a straw up to his lips.

"Thanks. Must have a frog in my throat."

"You need to eat, especially since I've just given you a shot of insulin. Cook's got some soft eggs for you."

"Tell Cook to feed them to the cat."

"You're gonna eat, old man!" says Kerwin, firmly. "Soon as you finish your story."

Hope winks at Kerwin. "You bet."

"Wild Buck was trying to teach us how to play ball with one spirit. In the game against Perry, he'd called time out and gone out to talk to Andrew on the mound, who'd just thrown a wild-ass ball that hit a Perry kid at bat. That's when all hell broke loose. The umpire, who was also a former U.S. Indian Agent, ran out to the pitcher's mound and claimed Andrew would have to come out of the game because he'd injured a player. Since the game was being played before an all-white crowd, the ump was afraid of being seen as partial to Indians. Remember, though, Wild Buck was also an elder who thought his job was guiding us, especially when we were playing all-white teams. Naturally, Wild Buck had a conniption, and the umpire threatened to march him off the field. But before the ump could manage it—Wild Buck might have been old, but he was a big burly sort—a private from Fort Riley came running up to the umpire. This was in 1898, mind you, and this fellow had a three-year-old newspaper clipping he took out of his satchel with all the latest baseball rule changes. I'm pretty sure it was a clipping from the *Cleveland Plain Dealer*. Back then, people hung on to newspaper clippings as if they were books, especially if they were baseball news. We found out later that the soldier was also an umpire who called games in his hometown. He showed Wild Buck that an infield fly rule had been established in 1895, and a number of other changes and game etiquette had been recommended.

"Wild Buck yelled at the private, saying that since Indians had invented the game of baseball he didn't think we ought to have to abide by rules written by white people from back east. For a moment it seemed as though Wild Buck Taylor was taking on the entire U.S. Army. To tell you the truth, I was a little afraid."

"Wait a minute," says Kerwin, looking up from Hope's medical chart. "I thought Abner Doubleday invented baseball."

"Nope."

"Who did then?"

"I just told you."

"Got any proof of that?"

"You're looking at it." Hope thumps his chest proudly with his shriveled forearm.

Kerwin puts his pen down for a moment then says, "Oh, okay, I see."

Hope can tell by the sound of his voice that Kerwin doesn't believe him. He hears the pen scratching on the pages of his medical chart.

"Where's your orange wig?" asks Hope.

"I wish you'd forget about that."

"Why?"

"I should never have pulled a stunt like that in front of the patients," says Kerwin. "I was way out of line." He sighs. "And I'll lose my job if it happens again. Then who'll diaper you?"

"Where's John Lennon, my-nurse-not-the-singer?"

Kerwin looks down at Hope and grins. The old man can be quite the cutup when he's in his right mind. "He enlisted in the Army. He's off this week getting a physical, going to Comanche ceremonies, sweats I guess, and preparing for boot camp."

"I did not know that," says Hope, inhaling deeply. "Missed him though. But I've heard it said many times that if America wants to defeat their enemies, they better enlist the aid of the Comanche."

They both chuckle. This is John Lennon's standard comeback about why America is losing the war in Vietnam: America doesn't yet have the Comanche on their side.

"John thought he should enlist before he's drafted," says Kerwin. "That way he'll have some choice as to where he'll be stationed before being shipped to Nam. You know, he's not as old as me."

"I thought he was older than you," says Hope.

"He acts like it," says Kerwin, rolling the adjustable table over to Hope's bed. "But I'm twenty-five and an *Okla Hannali* so I outrank Mr. John Lennon in all possible ways. Besides, I'm the only RN on the nightshift. John's twenty-three with an ex-wife and no baby—so he's out of deferments."

Hope studies Kerwin. From what he can tell, Kerwin is pretty tall for an *Okla Hannali*. He must be around six feet tall. The Choctaws who are *Okla Hannali* claim they originally came from the south. No one knows how far south the *Okla Hannali* lived before they traveled north to settle in the old Choctaw homelands along the Tombigbee River. Some say they came from Peru, others say the Gulf Coast of Mississippi.

"Where were you born?" asks Hope.

"Chickasha."

"That explains it," says Hope.

"What?"

"Why you're so tall. All the *Okla Hannalis* I've ever known were little bitty people."

"I'm tall because my father is Apache. My mother's people were *Okla Hannali.*"

"I was coming to that," says Hope. "Chickasha is a town where Indians from different tribes like to mix it up, so to speak."

"What could be better?"

Hope smiles. "Can't think of anything." He decides to change the subject. "Did I ever tell you about the time my teammates called me *Ohoyo Holba?* It was when we were making a movie."

"I didn't know you were in a film."

"Everyone who played for Miko Kings was in it. I was what you might call the star."

"No fooling? What was it about?"

"Baseball. I played the pitcher because I was a pitcher."

"What was it called?"

"*His Last Game.* I was dressed up like a Hollywood Indian, complete with long braids. The fellers gave me heck. They called me *Ohoyo Holba.*"

Kerwin looks at Hope for a moment. "What kind of *Ohoyo Holba* were you?"

"Not a good one, I'm afraid. In the old days an *Ohoyo Holba* was a respected person. They were givers who had multiple kinds of powers inside them. That's why a man would put on a woman's dress. By wearing the dress he was showing the world that he was in a state of grace, so to speak, a man without limitations. So no, I was never *Ohoyo Holba.* I had limitations."

At that Kerwin leans over and puts his hand on Hope's forehead.

"What kind of *Ohoyo Holba* are you?" asks Hope.

"I'm doctoring you. What do you think?"

"You're mighty good. Never felt better in my life."

Kerwin laughs.

"You know baseball is a game without limitations?"

"How so?" says Kerwin, putting a paper bib on Hope.

"Well, suppose your team went to a town to play ball and your pitcher got sick, or was cut bad on the way to the field. Indians wouldn't let a situation like that stop the game, so they'd pick up a player from the home team. That man would vow to play just as hard for the visitors as he would for his own team. This pick-up system helped with marriages too. Yep, old-timey Indians had a diplomatic solution for everything."

Hope raises his head and looks toward Kerwin. "Does your family know about you?" When Kerwin doesn't answer, Hope knows he hasn't told them. "Do you have a…"

"If you mean a boyfriend, the answer's no. It's not easy when you're *Ohoyo Holba.*"

"It's not easy when you're not," says Hope. "I know from personal experience that true love is hard to hold on to. When I was playing ball…"

Kerwin cranks up Hope's hospital bed. "I wondered when we'd get back to your favorite subject."

"Lucky for you I'm still alive to pass on these stories."

"Before I hear more of 'The Truth According to No Hands,' I'm gonna fetch your dinner. Don't go anywhere, I'll be right back."

Hope wonders where the hell he would go, even if he could. He raises up the sea horses and imagines that he still has hands. These days he lives only in his memories. Yet, recalling the experience that has surely killed him—kills him again each time he remembers. An irony he has learned to endure.

While she's not here in body, she is with him in spirit. That much he is certain of. Her echo settles into an armchair and she torments herself daily—mainly at sunset when the cicadas begin to sing. Her suffering yawns.

All past weeping.


Wild Buck Taylor continues staring down the soldier from Fort Riley. "Mister, the rules are the game in baseball," shouts the private.

Wild Buck doesn't move. "No they aren't," he says. "Baseball is a game with no limits!" The two men stare at one other and finally the private rolls up the sleeves of his uniform making ready for a fistfight. Then the Indian agent-turned-umpire haggles with both men, but no one can hear what's being said. Finally, Wild Buck shouts, still glaring at the soldier, "Andrew, grab some grass! Hope, you're up."

The makeshift ballpark erupts. The sight of Jones Academy's best hurler walking off the field to sit on the grass with the other Indians causes the Perry crowd to scream catcalls or whistle the Irish tune "Garryowen."

Others chant, *"Perry wins! Perry wins! Perry wins!"*

Someone blows taps on a bugle as Hope Little Leader, the sixteen-year-old Choctaw who's not a whit over five feet, six inches, jumps up off the ground and comes running onto the ballfield.

*"Perry wins! Perry wins! Perry wins!"*

For the white people living around Perry, Hope Little Leader represents just another sissy Indian boy who'll mature into a cattle thief. Many of Perry's townsfolk still hold grudges against the Comanche and the Osage for raiding their cattle herds. The Indians leave nothing behind but the dead carcasses of heifers as evidence of their moonlight marauding. It's another reason why Perry's players need a shave. They skip school each fall to try to protect the cattle herds from coyotes and Indians. Many of their players can't read or write, but the signs posted in town are spelled correctly: *R-E-D-S-K-I-N-S NOT ALLOWED IN PERRY AFTER SUNDOWN.*

Hope steps onto the mound just as a muscular white boy on third lets loose a war whoop. The white boy dances around the bag as if it were a fire. His mockery bolsters Perry's fans to greater insults.

*Blanket butts go home!*
*Blanket butts go home!*
*Blanket butts go home!*

Hope can see the game is over as far as Perry's team is concerned. But he isn't afraid of them, nor does he listen to their taunts. He's fixated on not letting his team down, or the old warrior Wild Buck Taylor.

Like every other boy at Jones Academy, Hope knows the stories about Wild Buck. There are rumors that he once rode with Buffalo Bill Cody, and that he finally had a bellyful of shooting dumb animals on the plains and came home to Choctaw Country.

There are other stories—that as a young boy, Wild Buck had ridden with Pushmataha against the Osage during *Hash Bissa,* Month of Berries. Pushmataha and the other Choctaw chiefs had offered a bountiful feast to the Osage if they would sit down and talk of peace between the two tribes. The Osage refused. So Old Push rounded up the bravest warriors, including Wild Buck, and they plundered the Osage buffalo provisions. Many warriors were killed on both sides, but the beleaguered Osage sued for peace with the Choctaws.

Supposedly the aging warrior still has the scalps he took, but he never discusses his past with the boys and they're too respectful to ask. Wild Buck says he wants to teach the boys lessons that will serve them a lifetime. Like proper hygiene. Proper care of teeth. Reading and writing. How to hone a billet of maple into a proper baseball bat thirty-five inches long, using a lathe, calipers, and a knob tool.

Now he's standing on the pitcher's mound, fuming. When Hope looks up at the low dense clouds, he fixes his eye on a hawk circling above them. One way or the other this game is coming to a quick end. A rainstorm is blowing in.

Wild Buck looks at Hope as if to say, "It's just the two of us facing down the white invaders." As he leans down, his voice is the calm before the rainstorm.

"On June 25, 1876, George Armstrong Custer and the 265 men

under his command lost their lives in the Battle of Little Big Horn. No one thought the Indians could take on the Seventh Cavalry and beat them flat. But they did. In 1805, Pushmataha led 350 Choctaw warriors in battle against the mighty Osage Nation. No one thought a bunch of Choctaw corn growers could whip a mighty Plains tribe— buffalo hunters at that. But nerve trumps brag every time, son. *This is* the battle at Little Big Horn. *This is* Pushmataha's finest hour. *This is* going way beyond your limits. Listen boy, there is no one I'd rather have standing here with me than you in this battle to show the good people of Perry what the Choctaw from Jones Academy can do."

As the other team continues to belly laugh, Wild Buck glances at Perry's runner, a hefty red-haired fella on third. "Make him eat dirt!" he says, walking off the field.

Hope nods and salutes. A holdover from his training at Hampton. He knows Perry's team expects nothing from him. They can't imagine what just happened. Wild Buck has compared him to the famous Choctaw, Chief Pushmataha. In the last three years, he's spent most of his time trying to run from principals and preachers at Hampton. Until recently, he continued that practice at Jones Academy. Since his mother's death, the only tasks for which he's exhibited any talents are pitching a ball and daydreaming about a black Indian girl named Justina, who up and left school for New Orleans. Now this persuasive old warrior-coach insists that he live up to his family name, Little Leader.

By now, Perry's man on third has completely let down his guard. Hope smells rain and breathes it in. He lets it fill him with all the possibilities that rainfall embodies. Life. Renewal. Rebirth. No one watching can tell that a change has occurred, but in that split second, Hope yields to the mystery that's been stalking him, a power he's aware of but cannot name.

What the spectators see is a slightly undernourished Choctaw boy from Jones Academy stepping onto the pitcher's mound. He looks up into the sky, winds up, and rears back. *Thmp.* Before the man on third can blink, Hope's ball hits the glove of his third baseman, Silman Zion. Perry's man dives toward third but Zion cuffs the tag. Hope goes on to strike out the next guy, and Jones Academy wins 3-2.

Afterwards, Wild Buck tells his players to go and shake the hands of Perry's baseball team.

At first the boys of Jones Academy, flush with victory in their stomachs, refuse, but Wild Buck is adamant. "We aren't just a baseball team—we represent the Choctaw Nation, and whether we win or lose we are the diplomats of our people," he says. Then he rushes around home plate and offers his hand to the soldier who brought the new baseball rules to the Indians. All nine ballplayers, the four alternates, and even the water boy scurry behind the old man like goslings trailing a mother goose. On their way across the field, heavy raindrops the size of silver dollars fall from the clouds, sowing mercy into the dusty parched earth of Perry.

The world dissolves in a dark downpour, a blue-green magnificence known by the Choctaw boys of Jones Academy as *Okchamali*.

Much later, on the four-day wagon ride back to Hartshorne, Wild Buck will ask Hope to sit up front in the buckboard with him. As the narrow dirt road snakes around one tall grass prairie after another, the old man strikes up a conversation.

"See the wind in the grass," says Wild Buck, pointing at the prairie. "It flocks together like a whole shining thing, only to be lost in our eyesight. We can't really see the wind—we only imagine how it looks. When the wind moans, we long to hold it with both hands, but it will slip right through our grasp."

Hope continues looking at the road ahead.

"Do you understand what I'm talking about?"

Hope tries to recall how he felt on the mound. "We cannot hold on to the wind, or to power," he says softly.

"At least not for long," says Wild Buck. "What did you see out there when you made that up-down movement? You know the one I mean. When you disappeared."

"Light," says Hope.

"What kind of light?"

"I don't know," he says, shifting uncomfortably in the buckboard seat. "Just light."

There were, of course, other things, but Hope is afraid to speak of them. A body stripped clean like the skeleton of a fish. A heartbeat, but only one. Memories falling away like bits of ash. A blinding flash from the Sun and then his wildest arm twirling around and around, seeming to bend light itself.

Wild Buck passes a gnarled hand thoughtfully over his chin. "Your uncle had the power, but he forgot that he couldn't hold it. After the Winfield Reds' season ended, it must have been in '96, Ahojebo went to his sister's place like always. When he found out she had passed on, he began to hunt for the man who'd taken her children. He found the reverend preaching at a country church east of Tulsa town. As he swung his ax again and again into the wooden front door of the church—he'd already chopped down the two pilasters holding up the porch frame—the reverend gut-shot him. By the time some of us got over to Tulsa, they'd buried Ahojebo out behind the church he was trying to destroy."

For a long moment Hope can't think of what to do. He'd been told his uncle was dead, but he didn't know how he died. Why hadn't Ahojebo come for him or his sisters instead of going after the preacher? Did he think they were already dead? None of this makes any sense.

Hope surveys the landscape. Here and there a stand of blackjack oaks dots the fields. Deer sign is everywhere. If he jumped out of the wagon and ran he could make it for awhile with just his knife and a little luck. He spots a wild potato root and some cactus blooming along the trail. That would keep him alive long enough until he could steal a horse. He should leap off the wagon. Run. Avenge his uncle's death. But he doesn't jump. Instead he looks anxiously up at Wild Buck.

"There's no point in running," says the old man. "Killing the preacher won't bring back your uncle. I told you because I thought you should know. What Ahojebo would say if he were here is that you should stay at Jones Academy. Learn to add and subtract. Read the newspapers. Harness your talent. The rest will take care of itself."

Hope nods thoughtfully. After a while he asks, "Did you ride with Pushmataha?"

"No," says Wild Buck. "But I feel like I was there from all the stories. My grandfather rode with Old Push against the Osage. He and I have the same name."

Another silence. Finally, Hope gets the nerve to ask, "Do I pitch like Uncle?"

The old man takes his free hand and rubs his chin again. "Ahojebo's arm was lightning itself," he says. "Ask me again, after you've hurled ten thousand balls from the mound. But that up-down look you made with your head, just before you released the ball, that was pure Ahojebo."


When Hope awakens, Kerwin is standing over him with a plate of scrambled eggs.

"Howdy," says Hope. "I thought you'd gotten lost."

"Not likely."

"Did I ever tell you what we had to go through to get the old ball-fields built in Ada?"

"Nope. And I won't hear another word from you until you've eaten something."

Kerwin begins spooning the eggs into Hope's mouth.

"Not so fast. I'm a slow chewer."

"How about you eat and I talk for a change?" says Kerwin.

"Deal."

"You know I play on a fast-pitch softball team?"

"What position?" asks Hope.

"Shortstop."

Hope swallows another bite. "The captain of the infield. Always admired shortstops. You're kinda tall for a shortstop. I'm thinking of the shortstop who entered the game in 1940 for the Brooklyn Dodgers."

"Pee Wee Reese."

Hope grins. Reese was small but fast.

"Your favorite shortstop?" asks Kerwin.

"Deacon Scott."

"Boston Red Sox. Quite an agile fellow for his day and time."

Hope scrutinizes Kerwin again. "Now, tell me the name of your mother's people?"

"Hachubbi. My mother's name before she married was Hachubbi."

"I bet we are related way back there," says Hope. "All ballplayers are, you know."

"John and I play on the same team—guess I should say 'played'—the Mean Red Machine."

Hope laughs and nearly spits out the last of his eggs. "Water."

"Don't laugh, we're pretty good," says Kerwin, putting a straw to Hope's lips.

"With a name like that you better be."

Kerwin wipes Hope's face and puts the glass on the table. "We've played every year for the past four years. Last summer at Wheeler Park we came in second."

"Ever play at the old baseball field in Ada?" asks Hope, regaining his composure.

"At Wintersmith Park?"

"No, the old field north of Main where the rodeos used to be."

"Nothing there now," says Kerwin.

"Too bad," says Hope. "Henri Day built the first ballpark there in 1904. But before he could outline the field, Lucius Mummy, our first baseman, told Henri he had to bring in an *Alikchi* to pray over the ground."

"What's an *Alikchi?*"

"A healer."

"Oh," says Kerwin. "I thought *Ohoyo Holba* was a healer."

"That's not his main job. Seems to me you've got several Choctaw words mixed up in your vocabulary."

"I know," says Kerwin. "I'm trying to learn."

Hope waves the spoon away. "Our *Alikchi* went around and around in circles about nineteen times until he had prayed the ground clean, and then he laid out the baseball field according to the four directions. A square within the circle. And that's where Henri Day built the first ballpark in Ada."

"I've heard of the square within a circle as being a medicine sign," says Kerwin, opening a jar of Gerber's baby food.

"Who's gonna eat that?" asks Hope.

"You."

"What is it?"

"Applesauce."

Hope raises his head and looks down at his toes. "Think I might be strong enough to stand up and pitch a ball," he says.

Kerwin ignores him. "That's your morphine drip talking. Open wide, Twinkle Toes. Polish off the applesauce and we'll decide if you can stand up."

Kerwin waits until Hope swallows the last spoonful then asks, "When did you come to Ada?"

The old man chuckles. "I took a job on a skunk farm outside of town. I must have been about eighteen or nineteen. I needed the work. In those days, skunk was supposed to be the new mink. A feller by the name of Dowd built the place and I went to work for his foreman,

Sam Lewis, raising and skinning skunks. One day I accidentally hit a mama skunk with one of my curveballs. Skunks are very sensitive about being hit. She sprayed me good."

"Did you bathe in tomato juice?"

"Sure did. Nothing works on the stink but time, though…I smelled pretty much like a pole cat for the two years I worked for Sam." Hope yawns. His hands are beginning to relax. They bother him less and less these days. A good thing. He knows his hands aren't really there, but they hurt just the same. At night they ache, and sometimes during the day his fingertips feel as if they're on fire.

"Did I ever tell you why I came to play for the Miko Kings?" asks Hope.

"Maybe, but tell it again."

"I met the genius of the outfit, Blip Bleen. He was skinny as an alley cat, with a scar on his right cheek. Some Ponca gal and him got tangled up and she'd cut him. But that was long before I met him. By that time he was the Miko Kings' manager. Playing manager. And I was pitching for Hartshorne, drooling to play for Miko Kings. I'd got word that they were interested in me, so I dressed in my best white Sunday shirt and pants and went over to Henri Day's house, where everybody knew Blip would be on Sundays. He was wearing coveralls, no undershirt. He was chopping wood for Ezol, Henri's niece. They were sweet on each other, though at the time I didn't understand why. I said, Mr. Bleen, I'd like to practice with the team. Know what he said?"

"What?"

"We don't."

Kerwin erupts in a loud laugh. Hope chuckles, yawns again, and closes his eyes, trying to hold on to his last thoughts. "I stood there not knowing what to say. It was like he was telling me off for asking a dumb question…"

Kerwin watches his patient drift off to sleep. Often the old man will raise his arms high in the air as if catching a fly ball. He wishes he'd known him when he was young and still had his hands. What a gift it would have been to watch the old-timers at the height of their athletic prowess. What a ballplayer Hope Little Leader must have been. He checks his watch. 10 p.m. Time to make the rounds. He turns off the light but leaves the door open.

Here too is another echo of baseball's childhood
memory in *Anompa Sipokni,* Old Talking Places.

The post office publicizes game times, the line-ups,
and merchandise.
Maple bats, $2
Ash bats, $1.50
Willow bats, a buck
Bass wood bats, 55¢

# 6

## The Vulgarians
### Indian Territory, June 1904

Henri Day looks across the site where two Choctaw teams have been meeting to knock the sticks since 1850. If there was ever a more sun-blistered, luckless, sticker-infested, snakey ballfield, he's never seen it. Yet this place annually draws hundreds of spectators for the legendary stickball match between Tobucksy and Sugar Loaf. Indians from across the Choctaw Nation save the entire year to barter on this one game. They place bets with blankets, horses, cows, pigs, calico dresses, fishing poles, and rifles. The grounds on either side of the playing field are a sea of merchandise.

Henri turns to his cousin Lonnie Johns and sighs. "If only we could stir up this kind of enthusiasm for our Indian baseball team back in Ada."

"Gotta allow gambling," says Lonnie Johns.

Henri winces. "Goddamn Naholla. Praise the Lord on Sunday. Then run off to another county to place their bets. I will never understand their pretense against gambling. They all love it so."

"You said it," says his cousin, biting into an apple.

Henri and Lonnie tip their bowlers toward the two Naholla men standing among a crowd of Indians. One of the white men is the Indian agent from Muskogee.

"He's got a big appetite," says Henri.

"Which one?"

"Our belov'd Indian agent."

"How much did he put down?"

"Fifty dollars." Henri folds his arms.

"Which team?" asks Lonnie Johns.

"Sugar Loaf by two."

"Figures," he says, tossing away the apple core. "You announced your intention to run for mayor?"

"The advertisement runs tomorrow in the *Ada Weekly News*." Henri watches as the tiny leather ball streaks past them.

*"Falamolichi! Falamolichi!"* screams Lonnie Johns.

"Throw it back!" shouts Henri in English.

Lonnie Johns looks at Henri ruefully.

"You want our Indian agent to pay up? Or don't you? That Naholla will pout like a child if you don't translate for him."

"You said it," says Lonnie Johns. "The Four Mothers…is the meeting still on?"

"Right after our Indian agent pays up and leaves. We want them to believe we're all just a bunch of folks out here, enjoying an afternoon of stickball."

"That's why *I'm* here," Lonnie Johns smiles.

Henri turns his attention back to the stickball game. For Indians, playing ball is in the blood, whether it's stickball or baseball. But so far, under his leadership, the Miko Kings have lost all their games. He's hired some good players, but he's missing some key element. These two teams, besides being fearless, play with one thing in mind: controlling the ball.

Stickball has always been a training game for warriors. The game teaches players the art of endurance. Each man wears a short deerskin breechcloth and a wide belt around his waist. Some of the belts are made of cloth, others are horsehide. Every player has a horsehair tail attached to the back of his belt. It is said that long ago, in order for the men to run and jump like deer, they wore tails cut from the hinds of proud stags.

Today the men are shirtless except for a mane of horsehair fastened around their necks, dyed blue and white for Tobucksy or yellow and green for Sugar Loaf. Players carry two *kapucha,* ball sticks, that are eighteen inches long and bent into an oblong hoop at the top. A leather string is webbed across the hoop of the stick to carry or throw the ball with. How do they do it? thinks Henri. He wishes he had their medicine.

He watches the leather ball flying high above the bobbing heads of the players. A swarm of arms and legs chase after it. For a split second, the only sound that can be heard is the knocking together of the *kapucha.* Henri shouts, *"Hokli, Hokli!"* to a Tobucksy player.

A Sugar Loaf runner catches the ball and throws it to a teammate who drops it. The crowd holds its breath while several players scramble after the ball. The red dust flies and Sugar Loaf captures the ball, knocking it across the goal for one point.

> *Himak nitak achukma abi hoke.*
> *Himak nitak achukma abi hoke.*
> *Himak nitak achukma abi hoke.*

"This day is good, we will win!" chant the supporters of Sugar Loaf.

*"Towa intonla achukma abi hoke,"* reply Tobucksy supporters.

"The ball is good and we will win it!" laughs Henri. "Ah me. What's the score?" he asks, turning to his cousin.

"Sugar Loaf by one," replies Lonnie.

Within minutes the players regroup and both teams score again. When the ball is tossed a third time, Malihoma from Tobucksy catches it. Henri watches Malihoma run across the field. All the other men from Tobucksy revolve around this player. Malihoma may be the oldest man on the field, but he still plays like his name. Red Storm. At least seven players from Sugar Loaf give chase, darting, tumbling, and battling Malihoma for the ball. He leaps over one fallen player, stomps the head of another, then hurls himself and the ball across the goal. His point ties the game.

*"Wah! Wah!"* shout the supporters from Tobucksy.

Malihoma is like watching glory, thinks Henri. Then he realizes what's missing from his baseball team. Heart. He needs someone like Malihoma. A ballplayer who's all heart could lead by example.

Henri turns to Lonnie Johns and shouts, "I think I have a solution to all our problems!"

"Not again," says Lonnie, grinning. "What?"

"We need to find a baseball leader like Malihoma."

"You said it."

The two men shake their pony bells and chant along with others from Tobucksy. *"Towa intonla achukma abi hoke."* Some of his cousins bang striking sticks together. The wives and sisters of the Tobucksy players trill like scissortail birds. The birdcalls are meant as a taunt, and Henri and Lonnie join in.

Sugar Loaf's women respond by running onto the field. Seemingly in unison, they turn and hike up their skirts to show off their buttocks to the Tobucksy supporters.

The crowd of men standing with Henri and Lonnie belly laugh at the women's antics. *"Wah, Wah.* Do us another favor. Show that again," shouts Henri. *"Hump-he,* I dare you."

This time the women of Sugar Loaf lift up the front of their skirts, a double insult to Tobucksy. Now Tobucksy women let out a dreadful war cry and run onto the ballfield, gathering rocks, water buckets, and broomsticks as they go. Some scream *"Ofi tek,"* bitch, as they rip off their aprons and attack Sugar Loaf's women.

Henri remembers thinking that he and Lonnie Johns should run like hell. But instead, he tells his cousin, "Never get in between Indian women when they're scrapping." He believes Lonnie Johns may have said, "Uh-oh," just as a woman from Sugar Loaf sprints across the field and bashes his cousin upside of the head with her broom.

When Henri finally wrestles away her weapon, she turns and attacks Mary, Lonnie Johns' sister, who was coming to her brother's defense. The two women deadlock in a war of petticoats, rolling around in the sticker grass. Henri pulls Lonnie Johns up off the ground and hollers, "We gotta get out of here!"

Together they watch as the *Alikchi* from Tobucksy runs past them with a bucket on his head. All around is chaos. Even the stickball players run off the field. It's widely known that a man's athletic prowess is useless against a woman's kick to his groin.

Henri can't remember what happens next, because a woman wielding a piece of firewood knocks him out senseless. Hours later, when he finally awakens in the back of his mother's wagon, she tells him that an elder, a female descendent of Pushmataha, put a stop to the pandemonium by gathering the head women on the ballfield and singing a call to prayer song.

Much to his mother's dismay, the fight disrupted the Four Mothers meeting, and Henri is blamed for the event that will forever be referred to as "Choctaw Intermission."

Three days later, Henri Day sits in the dining room of the Early Hotel, occasionally rubbing a wet handkerchief over the back of his neck. It still aches from the blow he took on the stickball field.

"Been reading about you in the newspaper," laughs J.C. van Meter, the hotel's owner and operator, as he pours Henri a cup of hot coffee. "Seems like Bonaparte has put it on the line."

"Goddammit, J.C." Henri looks up from the editorial page. "I'll say it again, Sugar Loaf misinterpreted the spirit of my challenge. And since when does the *Ada Weekly News* report on a Choctaw stickball game?"

"Since the Four Mothers Society has been causing so much grief, burning the Indian agent's outhouses, sand houses, and train depots all over Indian Territory. The newspapermen went to the game for the same reason Captain Tonnor, the Assistant Indian Commissioner, did. They went out there looking for the ringleaders of the Four Mothers Society. Surely you didn't think it was to see the famous match-up between Tobucksy and Sugar Loaf? Of course, it didn't help matters that Tonnor and the Muskogee Indian Agent both lost money on the game," says J.C., holding onto the metal coffee pot by its wooden handle. "While they may have forgotten to mention that little tidbit to the newspaper editor, they did remember the part about the Indian women tearing each other's clothes off. Reporting on things like 'Choctaw Intermission' only proves to the lily-white churchgoers that wild Indians can't manage their own affairs."

Henri mutters under his breath. "Goddammit. Choctaws are civilization its ownself!"

J.C. slaps him on the back good-naturedly. "Bad timing, that's all," he says, laughing.

"I guess so."

"Wanna slice of hot apple pie? We just took a fresh one out of the oven."

He opens the newspaper again. "No thanks."

"Ah, Henri, don't go reading Bonaparte's letter to the editor again. Forget about it."

When he doesn't answer, J.C. walks away to greet other customers coming in to enjoy an evening meal. Henri ticks off a list of personal disasters that have long swirled around him. For starters, he's unlucky in love. He's a widower. Been one for five years, ever since his dear wife Florence died of tuberculosis. People don't trust a man who won't remarry. Perhaps if he courted again? Henri pauses for a split second, wrinkles his nose at the prospect, and moves on down his bad luck list.

Then there's his deportment. People in Ada say he keeps his hair wild like a Baptist preacher on Sunday, but the rest of him is all wrong as well. They say he dresses like some fancy Easterner. Instead of wearing overalls and heeding the arbitrary dictates of ignorant farmers and nasty settlers, Henri prefers high-waist dandy pants and suspenders, a white shirt, silk tie, and a waistcoat. Even when riding his bicycle.

That's another thing. Since his first business venture, Pony Express Glue, failed to attract a single investor, he hasn't had the nerve to get back on a horse. The glue wasn't really made from ponies, but from seven old nags he bought at a sale and shot. Then he boiled down their hoofs, bones, and hides into a sticky jelly-like substance. The liquid stank so badly that people eight miles away in Fitzhugh protested. When the liquid didn't harden into a good adhesive, he and Lonnie

Johns had to plow the whole operation under, which explains why he rides a bicycle. Now, he shuns *isuba,* and will most likely have to avoid them the rest of his life. He's certain the horses will never forgive him for rendering them...well, for rendering them useless.

"More coffee?" asks J.C. gingerly.

Henri lowers the paper and grimaces. "Only a jigger," he says, raising his cup.

Why he ever thought of running for mayor of Ada is beyond him. He deeply regrets paying the filing fee to get his name on the ballot. He simply can't understand what possessed him to do it. Well, on second thought, he does know. He figured if he were mayor, he could influence the town council to allow baseball games on Sunday. Then he'd work to legalize gambling. His motives aren't all that self-serving. He had a plan to bring more jobs to Ada by setting up gambling booths at the ballpark. But since a citizen of his own tribe has come out against him in the race, it's likely he couldn't get elected town scavenger.

# THE ADA WEEKLY NEWS.

## June 23, 1904

### LETTER TO THE EDITOR

Henri Day is almost completely worthless, noisy, tedious, and slippery when it comes to paying for his meals at the Commercial Club meetings. He's foul-mouthed, pedantic, and self-aggrandizing about his Indian Baseball League, an association that will push for gambling in every business in Ada if allowed to flourish. He's incapable of speaking in a public debate without purpling the air with such language that would make a jailer faint. Witness what happened (because of his vulgar dare) during the so-called 'Choctaw Intermission.' However gifted by education or well-intentioned, if a man is ignorant of the customs and requirements of polite society, he risks exposing himself to ridicule. Therefore, I urge you to flatly reject Mr. Day's bid for mayor and instead vote for me on Election Day. I have humbly served this city as Alderman for the past three years. I will protect Ada's citizens from gamblers and all degrading influences.

Signed Leon Bonaparte
Candidate for Mayor,
Choctaw citizen, land leaser,
Ada businessman, and
Clerk, Ada Methodist Church

The essay is vile. And worse, Bonaparte's letter ran side by side with Henri's advertisement for mayor. How did Bonaparte get his letter published? Is the *Ada Weekly News* editor backing Bonaparte? If so, he'll take his business to the two other daily newspapers in town. Until today, Henri believed he had a good chance of winning. He belongs to all the right social clubs. He's become a member of the Commercial Club, an influential business association whose goal is to grow the town to twenty-five thousand citizens. He attends the Knights Templar meetings, though just the social hour gatherings, and last year he served on the town council. He also has name recognition. He donated several acres of his own land for Ada's first city park, and another small plot for the new postal office. Okay, part of the deal was that the Ada postmaster would have to hire his spinster niece, Ezol Day, but he simply had to get her out of the house and interested in something besides scribbling gibberish in her notebooks. Besides, he was right about her peculiar habits meshing with the routines of postal clerks. They tell him that she's never lost or misplaced a single piece of mail. Now, if he can only get his daughter Cora married off, he'll be free to concentrate on the really important matters: baseball.

Henri takes his last swig of coffee and fingers the newspaper. How to proceed? Bonaparte must want to be mayor pretty bad to concoct this kind of slander. He studies the commentary again. He does have to admit that on occasion he lets fly a curse word or two, but never in the company of women. Oh, perhaps every once in a blue moon he may have said something like "Daughter, please pass me the goddamn salt pork." Or, "I wonder if those goddamn Black Irish and those goddamn Chinamen are thinking to stay on in Ada once the railroads are built?" But outside of these rare instances with his daughter and his niece, and of course his dearly departed wife, he cannot think of more than a dozen times when he uttered English profanity.

He's certainly never spoken the kind of blasphemy Mr. Robert Burns of Spencer Academy used under the most dire of circumstances: "God damn the Irish, God damn the English, but God please bless the Scots."

He glances up just as J.C. is seating more customers. "Egad," he grumbles under his breath. "It's that mouthy Mrs. Atkins and her brood of do-gooders." Henri buries his face in the newspaper and pretends to be reading. He can't help but hear pieces of their conversation. Finally Mrs. Atkins' voice booms loudly across the room. "Henri Day is a child in a man's suit. A notorious layabout, and I've known his family most of my life. He wouldn't amount to a hill of beans if his mother, Mrs. Emma Day, didn't manage their farms and all the proceeds from cotton. She's a saint. So was poor Florence, his late wife. He'll never find another like her."

The airborne words of Mrs. Atkins hit him squarely in the chest and wound him deeply. "I wouldn't vote for him even if I could vote," she continues. "Remember that mess he made with the horses?"

She would bring up the horses. Henri lowers his newspaper and scowls at all the Naholla women seated at her table.

Mrs. Atkins glares right back at him. "I spotted that crop of hair of yours, Henri Day, as soon as I walked in. I just want you to know where you stand."

Folding the newspaper, he tosses a copper penny under the saucer. He picks up his bowler off the table and places it on his head. "No hard feelings, ladies," he says, tipping his hat toward them. "I will simply turn the other cheek."

Not to be undone, Mrs. Atkins nods politely. "My regards to Cora and Ezol."

Henri saunters out of the Early Hotel feeling slightly superior. He always does when he quotes the Bible to gossipy old hens. "When you've been insulted, take the high road, boys. Always quote the Bible to the wicked," Mr. Burns would say. "They need it most."

Henri smiles, thinking of Mr. Burns' advice. He enjoys the sun's final warm rays as he walks along the new boardwalk that stretches from Main Street all the way to Oak Street. He resolves to forget about his recent run of bad luck. He's buoyed by the progress all around him. His new Indian baseball team will benefit from all the new commerce in Ada. At six p.m., Main Street is still choked with farm wagons. Farmers often unhook their trace chains and leave their teams standing where they stopped. Every house has a peach and apple orchard, grape arbor, pigs, and a chicken coop. There's hay to be made here, he can just feel it. The whole town is alive and bustling and he and the Choctaws—and the Chickasaws—simply must remain at the center of it all.

He stares at the clear evening sky and realizes what must be done: find a manager to help build the Miko Kings. And then the League. A league of all Indian baseball teams will demonstrate that the people from different tribes can own something together. It will be the country's first inter-tribal business, an alliance that will spread across the whole U.S. Maybe even the whole goddamn continent.

"The Naholla can't take it away if it's owned outright by Indians," says Henri softly, under his breath. "And solvent."

Before going home for supper, Henri saunters down the newly built wooden sidewalk toward the Red Cross Store. He'd almost forgotten that Cora had asked him to bring home some fresh ground pork sausage. Just as he is about to step inside the store, he notices a terrible odor coming from the back alley closet. The closet badly needs cleaning. Henri wonders when the town scavenger last came by to take away the refuse.

"Damnation," says Henri aloud. What must we do to get people to do their jobs? he wonders. The man gets twenty-five cents a month for each back alley toilet he cleans. That adds up to around ten dollars a month. Surely the town ought to get better service for that kind of money. Besides, the scavenger knows he can dump the refuse out on my land as long as he plows it under.

"Ah me." Henri enters the dry goods store that carries clothing, building materials, and even has a meat counter. He signals the owner that he's taking a couple crackers and a slice of cheese. He places a store token in the money jar and looks around at all the new faces. The store is jammed with tie workers, men who cut lumber into railroad ties. But there are also carpenters, stonemasons, wranglers, doctors, and even three lawyers milling around. Last week the *Ada Star* reported that the population had tripled in three years to three thousand. But lawyers outnumber physicians twenty to eleven.

"Egad," he grumbles. "No wonder there's such a stink out back. The place is crawling with lawyer lice."

Henri nods politely when he sees Reverend Deaton, a Baptist and an affable sort of man. However, he wants to refrain from entering into his never-ending debate with Deaton about hogs running wild on Main Street, despite the city ordinance against it. Not today. The business with Leon Bonaparte has left him with very little patience. With allotment and statehood coming, Choctaws need to stick together more than ever. Why Bonaparte didn't talk to him first, before writing to the newspaper, is beyond him.

He wipes his brow. "Ah me," he says, absentmindedly. As he tries to get the attention of the butcher, a handsome woman walks over and stands next to him. She looks to be only a few years older than his niece Ezol, and she's unaccompanied. He wonders if she needs help, and conveniently recalls the etiquette training that was drilled into him at Spencer Academy.

"Repeat after me, men," Mr. Burns would say. "If you see a lady whom you do not know, unattended and in need of assistance, then by God, offer your services to her at once." Yes indeed, Henri says to himself. Every once in awhile a Presbyterian upbringing comes in handy.

"May I assist you, miss?" he asks.

"Thank you no, sir," answers the woman. "I'm just taking in the sights." She turns and extends a gloved hand. "My name is Nellie Bennett, second cousin of Basil Bennett, the town marshal."

Henri smiles, but doesn't immediately reply. He's just remembered the newspaper article. Under the circumstances, he's afraid his greeting may be out of place.

"And your name?" she asks.

"Please excuse my failing manners. I am Henri Day."

"Oh my, the famous gentleman. I've been reading about you in the newspaper."

Henri blushes. "Yes, I seem to be both unpopular and unlucky. A bad combination."

"But courageous," she says smiling. "You're building a ballpark, a baseball franchise, and you donated land for a public park that's named after your late sister."

"Ellen Park. How did you know?" asks Henri.

"My cousin is a big supporter of yours."

"Really?" Henri's heart is immediately lifted. "That's nice to know. I've backed the marshal many times in local public meetings." He studies the young woman as her eyes quickly dart around the store.

"Look at that gilded water faucet. It's just like the one I saw at the St. Louis World's Fair. I never expected to see it in Indian Territory," she blurts out. Then she quickly puts a gloved hand on her mouth. "Now it's your turn to excuse my bad manners, Mr. Day. I'm afraid I'm a foreigner here. A tourist really. I've come out west to visit my cousins, see wild Indians in tipis, and attend the circus that's coming to town."

Henri had been thinking of making a personal call on her until she began talking about coming to Indian Territory to gawk at wild Indians. Why are white people so interested in Indians in tipis? he wonders. It suddenly occurs to him that he's building a baseball park so people, many of them whites, can be entertained by watching Indians play ball. *Woe unto you, scribes and Pharisees, hypocrites!* "God hates a hypocrite," he mumbles.

"What did you say, sir?"

"Excuse me. I fear I mumble on occasion. What I said was that I was recently a tourist myself," says Henri. "My cousin and I visited St. Louis just this past May for the 1904 World's Fair. What a charming city."

"How marvelous! What were your favorite exhibits?"

"The Palace of Electricity, with all the new inventions. Think of it, Miss Bennett, just last year the Wright Brothers flew a contraption up into the atmosphere. We have gasoline-powered buggies. We can hear across great distances through the invention of the wireless telegraph. The world is changing."

"You are so knowledgeable, sir."

"Thank you. But I'm really only repeating what I read. And your favorite exhibition?"

"The Apache Geronimo. He was selling small pictures of himself. I bought one, and a small arrowhead that he had fashioned."

Figures, thinks Henri. The government likes to trot out Geronimo every goddamn chance they get. He's a living war trophy for the U.S. Cavalry at Fort Sill. He smiles politely as she continues talking about Geronimo. Yet he can't help but notice that Miss Bennett has lovely grey-green eyes, dark brown hair, a small frame—*and* she thinks he's courageous. However, he's forty-four years old, much too old for courting and for teaching a young woman from St. Louis that Choctaws arc civilization its ownself! But then again, he must not judge St. Louis people too harshly.

"Perhaps we could continue our conversation at another time. May I call on you and your family, Miss Bennett?"

"Certainly, sir. I'll inform cousin Basil that you intend to pay us a call tomorrow."

With that, Miss Bennett smiles and walks toward the door. Before leaving, she turns and says, "Until tomorrow."

Strange, he thinks. She bought nothing. Surely she didn't come into the store just to look at water faucets and pork sausage. Could she be one of his cousin Owana Joe's new clients? "Ah me," he says softly, pondering the absurdity of the twentieth century, with all of its dazzling inventions and contradictions. These days if the Naholla aren't trying to kill Indians out west, they're trying to marry Indians in Indian Territory. Or worse, they claim they *are* Indians. This year alone, a jillion white people have tried to register themselves as Choctaws or Chickasaws on the Dawes Rolls.

He looks around the store at all the new faces. Most of the immigrants can't tell a Choctaw from a Dutchman. Things are so mixed up these days that Owana Jo Harkins arranges marriages between immigrants and Indians. "Her livelihood is a complete scandal," he mutters.

"What's that, Henri?" asks the butcher.

"Ground a pound of sausage," he says. "Please, sir."

He gazes absently at the hog meat as it is ground up and bleeds onto the counter. Life is a series of contradictory opportunities. For the past five years, he and his mother have fought allotment. As part of the Four Mothers Society, an organization that boasts twenty-four thousand Choctaws, Creeks, Chickasaws, and Cherokees as members, they're opposed to having the government slice up their tribal lands into squares of private ownership. But lately Henri's growing increasingly worried that nothing they do will stop the allotment process. A few nights ago he had a strange dream, in which he saw a modern baseball field unlike any other. He decided it must be from the future. The sign on the stadium read *Chahta Hapia Hoke*. We are Choctaw. Out of all the turmoil of allotment there might still be opportunities for Indians—if only they'll act on them. That's how he hit on the idea of starting an Indian-owned baseball team and, eventually, an entire league. But so far the only board member is Lonnie Johns.

"Dear Lord, help us." Henri sighs, deeply. He digs in his pocket and hands the butcher four newly minted 1904 copper pennies. He briefly stares at the image on the penny, an Indian in a headdress. "Figures," he says.

A few steps out of the store, he feels someone place a hand on the back of his shoulder. "Prayer is good for the soul, Henri," says the cherry-faced Reverend Deaton. "The Lord heard you a moment ago. And he will answer. 'Pray to thy Father which is in secret; and thy Father which seeth in secret shall reward thee openly.' Matthew 6:6."

"Thank you, Reverend," says Henri, tipping his bowler. After the preacher is out of earshot, he mutters obscenities under his breath, straps the package of sausage to the back of his bicycle, and pedals home. He cannot see how a coin with an Indian in a headdress stamped on it is the answer to anyone's prayer.

The next morning around sunrise, Henri awakens to someone pounding on the back door of his house. By the time he rousts himself and opens the door, Marshal Bennett is shouting and is fit to be tied.

"Hell fire, Henri! We've got ourselves an emergency out on your prairie, outside of town. We've gotta get a move on!"

He quickly dresses as the marshal paces around the sitting room. He's never seen Bennett in such a state.

"I've had my quota of squalid dealings, but this is by far the worst. Before coming to fetch you, I rounded up two other aldermen. One of them is Leon Bonaparte. Now, I know you two are at odds, but I'm asking you to put your political differences aside. We need plenty of witnesses. A man's hanged himself from one of the blackjack oaks out on your pastureland. The rest you'll just have to see for yourself."

Henri throws his coat on as he jumps into the large wagon with the rest of the men. As Bennett drives his mules, the men sit quietly, waiting to find out what has happened. When they reach the outskirts of Ada, Bennett pulls the mules to a halt and turns to address them.

"It's another settler stray incident. You fellers know how it is. This time it's a white man and woman who have unlawfully trespassed on Henri's allotment land. But the worst of it is that the squatter has hanged himself after his wife found him having relations with a chicken."

Henri's shocked. He's never heard of such a thing. He wonders if he's misunderstood, but when he looks at the faces of the other men he realizes he must have heard correctly. Before anyone has a chance to speak, Marshal Bennett, who has just cut off a chaw of tobacco, continues. "Every three-legged, blind-in-one-eye mongrel is moving into Indian Territory, and I swear every one of 'em is a simpleton. Frankly, I don't know what we're gonna do if this continues."

Henri wonders who the "we" is, since the "settler" is on *his* prairie. *His allotment land*. Since when has Bennett started thinking this way? But then again, Marshal Bennett has been a good friend to the Choctaws and Chickasaws. Henri looks at Leon Bonaparte, and a feeling of great sorrow passes between them. Perhaps they both need to re-learn the lesson their ancestors learned when the Europeans first came into the homelands: if Indians don't stick together, they're doomed to be overwhelmed by the Naholla.

The marshal snaps the reins and the mules mosey along the bumpy road lined with blackjacks. Finally they reach Henri's prairie, a small plateau covered in prairie grass, surrounded by a dense forest. In the distance they can see half a dozen buzzards circling in the sky. The air smells sickly sweet, even a quarter-mile away. Henri recognizes the smell as death. The shack is rough and, from the look of things, it was thrown up in a few hours. In the tree next to the shack hangs a skinny dead man, his body already swarming with flies. A woman with stringy blond hair sits on a fat tree log, cut down to serve as a bench outside of the shack. She acts as if she doesn't see them.

Henri and the others get out of the wagon and cover their noses. The dead man is all eyes and ears. Blood leaks steadily out of his nose, as if it were broken shortly before he hanged himself. The man might be fifty, maybe younger, it's hard to tell now. He has a bluish-yellow face; his tongue is swollen and protrudes out of a mouth furred by red dirt and bits of grass. His death smell inundates the trees, the purple sage-brush, and the milkweed. Everything.

The bloated body gives a twitch and sighs. Bennett picks up a stick and pokes the hanged man in the stomach to see if—incredible as it seems—the man might still be alive.

"Intestinal gas, that's all," says Bennett. "Odd how it takes nine months for us to be born, but only seconds to die." He turns back to the men. "The way I understand it, these two been looking for a vacant place to squat. Drifted from town to town, living off charity, until they stumbled across Henri's land. She says she caught him in the act when she rushed into their shack to investigate the noise. I shot the hen right after she told me what happened."

"What were you doing way out here that early in the morning?" asks Henri.

"Huntin' panther," says Bennett, spitting his chaw on the ground. "Yesterday Mrs. Timmons said a panther got her billy goat. She said it ran east in the direction of the plateau, so I came out to track it before dawn. Some time after daylight, I heard this squalling and bawling, and rode over to investigate. The old man had apparently tried to strangle her to keep her from talking, but she managed to escape. She's got bruises on her neck."

Bennett lowers his voice. "Everything's eggs in the coffee, boys. We gotta get her out of town and quick. Decent people shouldn't be exposed to these nasty foreign ways."

They all agree. Alderman Tom Johnson offers to buy the woman a railroad ticket out of town. Henri and Leon are appointed to burial duty. When Johnson suggests they ship her all the way to St. Louis, she begins protesting loudly. Her words might be English, but to Henri they sound like, *"Attentincion, Attentincion, beef and shoes gatt faa."*

Bennett picks up the woman, throws her over his shoulder, and plops her into the wagon, all the while translating her foul curses. *"Listen, listen, you beastly Jews, get fucked."*

Henri is aghast. What does this woman have against the Hebrews? All of the history lessons he learned at Indian boarding school began with the victory of the Israelites over the Egyptians, Exodus 14:26. Mr. Burns would begin: "And the Lord said unto Moses, Stretch out thine hand over the sea, that the waters may come against upon the Egyptians, upon their chariots, and upon their horsemen."

When Henri looks over at Leon Bonaparte he can tell he's praying softly in Choctaw. Actually, Leon is chanting for the dead man's spirit to find peace on the other side—and for the crazy woman to find peace anywhere but here. Henri doesn't bother translating for the white men. It's none of their business. Besides, only Choctaw words can soothe the land and put to rest violent abominations.

The foreign woman ignores Leon's prayers. She turns to the white men and pleads, "I work myself. I work myself." Her English is meager, but more understandable now that she's calmed down. "In Prussia, I work the man. In America, everyone whores. Same, same," she says, placing her hand over her heart. "Not send me away."

Her face is shiny with sweat. She twists a small strand of her blond hair around her finger, and points to Henri. "Come," she says.

He shakes his head no.

She turns to Leon. "You."

She stares at the two Choctaws as one might stare at a map, trying to decide which path is the correct one. When it is clear neither Indian is willing to be her guide, she turns to Alderman Johnson. "Come you *gatt faa*."

The marshal doesn't wait for any more appeals, but snaps the reins, and the wagon lunges forward. He shouts to Henri and Leon that he'll send a horse and rider back for them.

"We'll see that she gets out of town safely," shouts Alderman Johnson, over his shoulder. "She's as good as gone."

In no time, the wagon is out of sight. Leon Bonaparte walks over to Henri. He says another prayer in Choctaw. This time Henri takes off his bowler. Bonaparte asks Henri to forgive him for writing the letter to the editor. He explains that he's a Christian and that he's given up the old ways. "I can no longer support gambling in any form. That's the main reason I wrote the letter," says Bonaparte.

"I understand," says Henri, wiping his face with his shirtsleeve. "I've attended church all my life."

Bonaparte gives him a stern look.

"Judge not, lest ye be judged," says Henri.

Leon starts to protest, but Henri cuts him off. "Let's just say that I'm more of a 'both-and' kind of fellow. I'm a Christian—of sorts—and I also respect Choctaw beliefs. Now take baseball, for instance. To some, that's church."

"Baseball is not supposed to be just a leisure-time activity," says Leon.

"Oh, so you do believe in our people's old ways," says Henri.

Leon gives him a long hard look. "I'll retract my words about you."

"I'd very much appreciate that," says Henri, looking around at the mess the foreigners have made of his land. Then he recalls another one of Mr. Burns' sayings: "Anyone who makes us suffer is undoubtedly suffering, too."

Leon interrupts the silence. "I want you to know that I'd make a better mayor than you."

"I don't doubt that. All I was really trying to do was to get people interested in going to the ballpark and watching the games. I thought gambling would bring them in."

Leon laughs. "You need good ballplayers, not gamblers. That's how you get people to buy a ticket to a baseball game. You've got good ideas, Henri, but poor follow-through. Why don't you talk to my cousin, Napoleon Bonaparte, third baseman for Hartshorne? He's got quite an arm. He says they've got a fellow over there named George Bleen, "The Blip," who's the best slugger in Indian Territory."

"We need good hitters," says Henri, extending his hand. "Say, you wanna become a board member on our Indian League Baseball Association? I'm giving away shares at this point, to drum up interest in the league. But later, we're going to sell shares. Any Indian with a dollar can own part of the league. We've based our model on the Four Mothers Society."

"Maybe," says Leon. "But first let's put that one to rest," pointing to the squatter hanging from the tree.

"Ah me," sighs Henri. "Notice who is digging the grave, and who is riding to the train station."

"They're not taking her to the train station," sniffs Leon. "I can tell you that much."

"Well, that's what they said."

"Oh for Pete's sake, Henri! You're always being caught unaware. I bet you they drove her straight to the Corner Saloon. You know as well as I that they keeps floozies out there. Surely you don't believe that Bennett just happened to be out here hunting panther on the prairie, when he heard a Naholla gal in distress?"

"You can't bet on anything, remember?" snaps Henri. "You're against gambling."

"You know what I mean. Why do you think Bennett left us here to dig the Naholla's grave? Bennett's more oily than most," says Leon. "Always has been."

Henri picks up the shovel that Marshal Bennett threw off the wagon. He digs into the dry earth and tries not to curse. He doesn't want to lose his temper while hollowing out a body's grave. That would be truly sinful. He needs a pick ax; the ground is as hard as granite. He wonders if he's always been this gullible.

"Panther hunting, indeed," he mutters. Of course, once upon a time, he had seen a she-panther padding down Broadway Street in the wee hours of morning. By now he figures all the panthers have lit out for higher ground, somewhere safe from the Naholla. What is Bennett really up to?

Leon begins gathering large rocks to place on top of the grave. The rocks will hopefully keep the coyotes from digging up the dead man. For the longest time there is silence on the pastureland, nothing but an occasional gust of wind to mark the passing of time. The buzzards are moving closer now, occasionally landing near the hanging tree. Leon hisses and throws a rock that hits a bird squarely on the head, causing it to take flight. Once the hole is deep enough, the two Choctaws head to the tree and cut the poor man down.

Henri is the first to break the silence. "As soon as we plant him, can you tell me more about The Blip?"

# THE ADA WEEKLY NEWS.

## July 1, 1904

### BASEBALL

Now that construction on Miko Kings' field has been completed, innovator Henri Day announced today he's adding slugger Blip Bleen as player-manager for his fledgling team. Bleen brings with him three players: third baseman Napoleon Bonaparte, rookie first baseman Lucius Mummy, and veteran catcher Albert "Batteries" Goingsnake. Day has found it necessary to find weekly co-sponsors for the baseball games, so he's added a gigantic 80-foot billboard behind home plate, to be painted weekly with the sponsor's name and the price of their goods. Also, it's a good safety measure on Day's part, considering some of the wild pitches have been known to kill spectators' kids. After last Saturday's explosive 10-0 loss to Roff, Henri Day has added another sign at the entry of the ballpark:

1) No intoxicating liquors allowed on the grounds.

2) No profane language allowed.

3) Betting strictly forbidden.

4) Grandstand privileges 10 cents extra.

5) Absolutely no prostitution in the ballpark.

6) Horses and carriages admitted on the grounds free of charge.

7) Admission 10 cents for adults, 5 cents for children.

8) Killing of umpire absolutely prohibited.

This should convince Adans that Day is truly against gambling.

And here too is another echo of baseball's childhood
memory in *Anompa Sipokni*, Old Talking Places.

He threw Spitballs
Dopers
Out-Drops
Fist-Sockers
Inshoots
Up-Downs
and Curves.

He threw Twisters and
Cyclones
Tornadoes
Tropical Storms
Whirlwinds
Typhoons
Gale Winds
Nor'easters
A Gentle Breeze.

He threw Varmints and
Robbers
A Tempest in a Teapot
Freaks
Jack London's Call of the Wild
Snapping Turtles
A Red Hen
Elephants and Donkeys
The Wabash Cannonball.

He threw Racetracks and
Beer Kegs
Broken Treaties
Casinos
Missionaries
The Civil War.

He threw Hell at them
And Paradise.

When there was nothing left
he threw himself, and strolled off the mound
disappearing into a three-letter town
named Ada.

# 7

## The Lord and the Center of the Farthest

### Ada, Oklahoma, September 2006

Nothing for three months. I haven't written a word since Ezol Day disappeared from my life. I have, however, traveled to the archival libraries at the Baseball Hall of Fame Library in Cooperstown, New York, the D'Arcy McNickle Center in Chicago's Newberry Library, and Hampton University. All on the instructions of a ghost. I must be mad as a hatter. But, then again, I can't think of a more interesting way to spend the small inheritance that Grandmother left me.

Hampton was originally founded in 1868 as a Normal school to educate newly-freed blacks during Reconstruction. In 1877, the school, under General Samuel Chapman Armstrong, began a program to educate Indians. The program continued for forty years before it petered out due to lack of federal monies and Foreign Mission Board support, among other reasons. It was eventually renamed Hampton University and became one of the country's black colleges.

I did manage to track down a picture of Hope Little Leader with a trombone under his arm, supposedly taken at Hampton in early 1896. Miss Smith, a secretary at Hampton, kept careful notes about the Indian students there. Hope's file had a note penned at the top of it saying that he was a habitual runner, always trying to escape. Smith also noted that Little Leader had exhibited "strong feelings" for a young Negro woman named Justina Maurepas, a teacher's aide, and that he had been forbidden to speak further with her.

For a time, Hope was housed in the Wigwam, the Indian boys' dormitory. He seems to have been the subject of at least two Wigwam

Council discussions in which it was argued that he should be sent back to Indian Territory. He was also cited for leaving the school grounds after taps and for bringing the moral standards of Indians down to a new low. His record at Hampton ends in 1897, and no further mention of him is made after that.

I found several records about the Four Mothers Society in the archives, some written in Choctaw that I could not translate because I'm not fluent enough. According to *And Still the Waters Run* by historian Angie Debo, the Four Mothers Society was an organization against allotment made up of the largest southeastern tribes, the Choctaw, Chickasaw, Creek, and Cherokee. A forerunner of our political action committees. The Seminoles are part of the "Five Civilized Tribes," but not part of the Four Mothers Society, for reasons that are unclear to me. These five tribes were all originally from the southeastern states before forced removal to Indian Territory.

The organization began around 1895 and lasted through 1915, roughly the same length of time as the heyday of Indian Territory baseball. Both the baseball teams and the Four Mothers Society disappear from historical documents after the First World War begins.

During the turn of the century, however, the Four Mothers was a vibrant, vocal organization opposing the allotting of their lands. Members supported the work of the Four Mothers with monthly dues ranging from a dollar a month for a man, twenty-five cents for a woman, and five cents for children. Debo writes that the Four Mothers Society sent "frequent delegations to Washington to secure a restoration of the old ways, and employed a white man representing himself to be an attorney to secure legislations to that effect." I think I understand why Ezol asked me to research the organization. Not much is known about the inner workings of the society, yet the Day family was heavily involved in the activities of the group, often arranging their meetings at stickball games and tribal baseball games. Interesting that the best place to organize was at a ballgame.

In a way, Henri Day's Indian baseball league seems to be a twin model of the Four Mothers Society. Organize the Indian baseball teams into a franchise. Sell shares of the franchise to raise money and build it into a powerful league. It seems that Indians in the southeast had been organizing inter-tribally to play ball long before the Europeans ever arrived. According to historical accounts and archaeological reports, there are old ballfields along river bottoms and next to the mound sites. So Henri Day's new baseball league was based on something very old.

Next on the list was to find John Lennon. Was there a connection between the most famous Beatle and American Indians? I went to the local library and tried to connect the Beatles' early music with American Indian causes. But I didn't turn up anything. Perhaps John Lennon had become friends with an Indian baseball player while living in New York City. I sat for one entire day reading all the online articles I could find about John Lennon but saw nothing relevant to Oklahoma. That evening it finally hit me—how could Ezol Day have known about John Lennon in 1907, unless she had been traveling back and forth in time...*before.*

The thought so unnerved me that I went straight to the liquor cabinet and poured myself a scotch. I sat completely still at my desk, watching the ice cubes melt and wondering what Ezol wanted of me. Had we somehow met before? Or would we meet, say, next week? Or next month? And the reason I couldn't remember is because I'm here now, in the past, and our initial meeting hasn't happened yet? I took a drink and pondered what I don't know about quantum physics. Then I got mad. Why was I following the orders of a ghost who comes and goes as she pleases? What does she want from me anyway? Downing the rest of my drink, I decide to take charge of the investigation. While I'd read through the loose contents of the mail pouch, I'd never untied Ezol's journal and sorted through her papers. As long as she was around to talk to and ask questions of, I hadn't bothered. Besides, I'm against reading other people's journals when they're...still around. Now that she's disappeared, her private thoughts are fair game.

I take her journal into the living room, delicately remove the ribbon, and begin lifting the pages out one at a time. Some of the pages are so brittle that I must slide a sheet of copy paper beneath them to prevent them from breaking apart in my hands. I place each yellowed page on the floor and begin ordering them by date and place. The process takes several hours of painstaking work. When I finally begin to read her words aloud, Ezol Day pops out of the pages of her journal—not as a spirit but as a child, and later still as a young, enigmatic woman who penned her own history.

My name is
3zol

We was all borned over there in Doalsville. Mrs. Leflore said it is not proper English that I learned.

FANCY is somewhere crying for me.

The Prince and the Birds.

(270)

in his way home; and should you think him as amiable as I do, I will consent that he shall be your husband as well as mine, which you know is agreeable to the laws of the prophet. If on the other hand, he is no more, I shall continue, by your kindness, in safety here; till I can acquaint my royal father with my situation.'

The princess of Ebene heard Badoura's story with wonder, and pity. When she had finished her narrative, Haiatalnefous embraced her, saying, ' I do not blame your sorrow, unfortunate princess ; it must needs be great for the loss of a husband, so accomplished, as you describe Camaralzaman ; I will keep your secret : and shall be glad, by every means in my power, to alleviate your grief.' From this time the most perfect friendship took place between the two princesses ; and Badoura became, every day, more esteemed by Armanos and his people, conducting the affairs of the kingdom with great ability and success.

While these things passed in the island of Ebene, Camaralzaman remained with his friendly gardener impatiently waiting for the time, when he should be able to set forward in search of his beloved Badoura. One morning, when he was preparing to go to work, the gardener prevented him, saying, ' This day is a great festival with the idolaters, on which account, they will not suffer mussulmen to work. I will go to the port and as the time approaches, in which the ship sails to Ebene, I will secure you a passage in it. But I would advise you to continue here; and amuse yourself in the garden till I return.

The prince pursued the advice of his host. While he was reposing himself, under a tuft of trees, indulging his melancholy reflections, he was disturbed by two birds, fighting, and making a great noise very near him. In a little time one of them fell down dead, and the victorious bird flew away

In a short time, two other birds came and pitched themselves one at the head, and the other at the feet of the dead bird. After seeming to express much concern, they dug a grave with their talons, and interred the defunct. This done, they flew away . but returned in a few minutes, bringing with them the victor bird, one holding a wing in her beak, the other a leg ; the prisoner all the while screaming most piteously, and

42                    *EVANGELINE,*

Soon was the game begun. In friendly contention
   the old men
Laughed at each lucky hit, or unsuccessful ma-
   nœuvre,
Laughed when a man was crowned, or a breach
   was made in the king-row.
Meanwhile apart, in the twilight gloom of a window's embrasure,
Sat the lovers, and whispered together, beholding
   the moon rise
Over the pallid sea and the silvery mist of the
   meadows.
Silently, one by one, in the infinite meadows of
   heaven,
Blossomed the lovely stars, the forget-me-nots of
   the angels.


Thus passed the evening away. Anon the bell
   from the belfry

Rang out the hour of nine, the village curfew,
and straightway
Rose the guests and departed ; and silence reigned
in the household.
Many a farewell word and sweet good-night on
the doorstep
Lingered long in Evangeline's heart, and filled it
with gladness.
Carefully then were covered the embers that
glowed on the hearth-stone,
And on the oaken stairs resounded the tread of
the farmer.
Soon with a soundless step the foot of Evangeline
followed.
Up the staircase moved a luminous space in the
darkness,
Lighted less by the lamp than the shining face of
the maiden.
Silent she passed through the hall, and entered
the door of her chamber.

*Of wearing nice clothes.*

Fola imisito or mayhaw. Mrs. deFlore
says May apple.
alikti, hofantit taha. Grown up.

aye tree

Aichna, Alas
~~Doaxland~~ Indian Orphanage, 1 March 1888
Day 100

I count the days until I go back
home to Doaksville.

Aichna, Alas
~~Good~~ Land Indian orphanage  30 October 1888
Day 340

"~~Too~~ country," is the reason Uncle gave me
when he came to inquire after my habits
of learning to speak and write and read
English. I protested asking him why I could
not have ~~stayed~~ with Aunt Fancy in ~~Doaksville~~?
~~Doaksville~~? Dear Aunt Fancy taught me
everything. In the shake tent when the
alikchi healed me from the attack by the
iti mishkin, it was Aunt Fancy who
~~took~~ me ~~to~~ be healed. I can still see
the eye true but alikchi winnowed
the branches and sucked out pieces
of its bark from within that plagued
me. When he blew them upwards
into the winds I felt relief.
Uncle would hear none of this.
He severely criticized Aunt Fancy
and said, girl, learn to read and
write and speak fully in English,
That is all we ask. Until then, you
may not go home to Doaksville.

I said to Uncle. I speak.
You speak.
We spoke.
~~to apela. Help~~
Sia aplla. Help me.

Aichna, Alas
Good Land Indian Orphanage, 20 June 1889
Day 720

Sookie Bob and I have today been ~~severly~~ severely
reprimanded. The incident began when we found
ourselves outside in the late afternoon all alone.
I ~~do not~~ know ~~where~~ the ~~others~~ were. Unaccustomed
to being on our own, we walked down to the creek
a half mile from the girls dormitory. The distance
could be farther, but I am certain it is not a
mile as Mrs. Beemer said. We had taken off our
work dresses and walked into the creek. I felt more
joy than I have known in the longest while, as
a cool spray of water landed on my face and
bare arms. Sookie Bob used the palms of her
hands to push the water toward me. I heard
myself laugh loudly. Then she laughed too. It was
a very hot afternoon and we delighted in being
completely wet. I suppose this suggests to the
civilized mind that Choctaw girls are savages
still, if left to our own devices. The girls of
our school are taught to sit quietly and learn
good habits of sewing and cooking. Good care
of teeth and to recite long passages in the
Bible. (To always be fully clothed.) When we
returned to the dormitory there was a loud
commotion and Mr. Gibbons, the superintendent
of the school was aggrieved that we had
left the others and gone off alone.
Sookie Bob was charged with the infraction,
as she is older than me. For this I am truly
sorrowful as we are on outhouse duty for the
next two weeks. 			Si apela. Help me.

Aichna, alas
Good Land Indian Orphanage, 1 June 1890
Day 1070

There is but one subject on which all lecturers agree in
this region, that is to encumber our minds with a strong
belief in the Lord almighty (and his miracles.)

... Then spake Joshua to the Lord in the day when
the Lord delivered up the Amorites before the children
of Israel, and he said in the sight of Israel, Sun,
stand thou still upon Gideon; and thou Moon, in the
Valley of Aj'a-lon.

And the sun stood still, and the moon stayed,
until the people had avenged themselves upon their
enemies. Is not this written in the Book of Jasher?
So the sun stood still in the midst of heaven,
and hasted not to go down about a whole day.
And there was no day like that before it or
after it.

Joshua 10: verses 12,13 (and one sentence of verse
fourteen for my own use.) Aunt Fancy said
Old Man Spivey once doctored the storm by cutting
the wind in half. If Old Man Spivey can doctor
a storm then the sun must surely have stood
still for Joshua and the Lord. Time is at the
mercy of the speaker.

Si' upela. Help me.

Aichna, Alas
Good Land Indian Orphanage, 12 September 1894
Day 2545

Uncle is a strangely proper man, cheerful,
and yet always quoting dark passages
from the Bible. His eyes are the same
brown color as his hair and he has a
way of turning them swiftly and holding
them on a person, or an object as if lost
in contemplation. I long to have no
inhibitions of looking squarely at a man
or a woman, when I am speaking.
Mrs. deFlore has long repeatedly warned
me of this unpleasant habit. I strive to
be like the other girls. Mrs. deFlore has
assured me that there is nothing, that
ails me and she forbids that I mention
the eye tree again, so help me God!

$$1 \text{ plus } 1 = 4$$
$$1 \text{ plus } 1 = 4$$
$$1 \text{ plus } 1 = 4$$
$$1 \text{ plus } 1 = 4$$

My mother plus my father equals 4,
accounting for my sister and me.
My sister and I are palokta humma.
Split red. Twins. Therefore numbers
may split and remain unaccounted
for as in one plus one equals four.
Zero is a circle filled with thousands
of numbers and verbs hidden inside it.

Numbers have lives inside of lives. With the help of the eye tree I often see patterns I cannot explain. The numbers 4, 9, and 14 are patterns and I see them everywhere. But in other ways the eye tree distracts me and this is how I get into trouble— I become immune to my surroundings.

How I miss my Aunt Fancy. Until I was moved to Good Land Indian Orphanage she was all that I loved since Father's disappearance and the passing of dear Mother and Sister. I admit that I did not know Mother or my sister Evangeline, but I love them just the same. Both passed into the next world without me. Sometimes I see Evangeline standing a few feet from me. She is a torch of light against the darkness. Come along, she says, but I hesitate and do not follow her for fear I cannot find my way back. Uncle does not like me to speak of Sister or Mother. But when I press him he will tell me about Mother's beautiful voice and how she loved to sing. I am told Evangeline and I lay side by side in the same bed until she followed Mother to the next world. Aunt Fancy said that Sister's tiny footprints could be seen on the quilt trailing after our dear Mother. I believe Evangeline was buried under Aunt Fancy's house.

When I am lonely I look in the big mirror in the dormitory because we look exactly the same, my twin and I. So I am told.

Si apela. Help me.

27 April 1897

D. Appleton Com.
243-253 Wabash Ave.
Chicago, Ill.

Gentlemen,
        Please send to me, as soon as possible, books
as per enclosed list. Send them whichever way is
cheapest, and include transportation from Chicago
to Indian Territory in the price of books.
Transportation charges must not appear on the
bill. Send bill in triplicate, giving best discount,
and a check will be forwarded upon receipt of
books.

Very respectfully,
Mrs. Sara Anderson LeFlore
Presbyterian Church and
Good Land Indian Orphanage
Good Land Mission, Indian Territory

Post Script. Although highly unusual, I am asking
for your counsel about other books that might be of
interest to a young Choctaw woman at Goodland
whom we believe to suffer from "genius symptoms."
When she arrived here in 1887, she was eight and
barely uttered words in her own tongue. However,
she could draw, and with patience and God's love,
we were able to teach her to speak proper English.
After a year, she began to read and write clearly
in English and much beyond her youth, which aston-
ished everyone at Good Land. Now at age eighteen,
she amazes us with multiple reckonings of numbers.
She excels in the subject of writing, and is now
beginning to read in French, thanks to a young
teacher and missionary who passed through our
country. I have written to the Executive Committee

of Home Missions Presbyterian Church, U.S., begging
that they send all the science books they can in order
to keep the young woman's mind occupied, as she has
nervous habits when she is idle. Please send to me
any list of titles that might be of interest to our
needs at Good Land, and to the needs of the student I
have described.

The Expanse of Heaven - Proctor
The Ministry of Flowers - Friend
The New Army Drill Regulations for Infantry - French
The Autobiography of the Earth - Hutchins
First History of Rome - Sewall
First History of Greece - Sewall
Ocean Wonders - Damon

Aichna, Alas
Good Land Indian Orphanage, 9 September 1899

Aunt Fancy died.

I was allowed to go home to Doaksville to see her
before she passed. She lay in a coma for two weeks.
After the funeral, but before I was taken back to
Good Land, Aunt Fancy, appeared to me in the room
where she died. She was young and beautiful and
wore a blue and white checkered scarf tied around
her head. She stood at the foot of the bed where
I was sleeping, and I awoke to see her presence
in the room. I held out my hands to her but she
didn't approach me. She said, "I'll be back in
seven days." Then she disappeared. I marked the
days on a stick because there was no paper.
On the seventh day, she did not appear.
I cried and cried. However, it was then I began
to question the nature of her day. Why should
Aunt Fancy's time be the same as mine in Doaksville?
I began to think about this.
I added it up from what I could still see in
the eye tree. I began to think about Joshua
in the Bible. It seemed to me that time was
not the same for the Jews on the day when
Joshua told the sun to stand still, and the
sundial did not change. The place where
Aunt Fancy bides her time waiting for seven
days to pass is not the same as our time.
There must be many locations in time and
languages. I will make an effort to prove it.
Si apela. Help me.

Good Land Indian Orphanage, 12 December 1899

Uncle. Amoshi. Sir.

When am I going to be allowed to leave for Doaksville?
Am I not now speaking, and reading and writing
in English? What's next?

Elle est seule. Appeler son Isole. Après tout
il y a seulement un dimanche. Isole est un
bon nom pour elle.

Ome. Wicked French!

Si apela. Help me

Aichna, Alas
Good Land Indian Orphanage, 1 October 1900

Even among the damned, President McKinley
will look bad, I overheard Uncle say to our
elders Mr. McCann, Mr. Gibbons, and Chief Smallwood.
I am told it is not proper to write such words.
Much less to speak them.

Si apela. Help me.

Ada, Indian Territory

10 October 1900

This past week Uncle, after having moved me from Good
Land to Ada, decided that he would take Cora and me
north to a baseball game over in the Cherokee Outlet. A
wild place, Orlando was. In 1891, only a switch stop.
Now, said Uncle, at least there is a depot. As he remembered it, there was only a cleared wide spot. We got off
the train and were to take a stagecoach to Stillwater,
where we were told a great crowd would gather to watch
the two Indian ball teams battle it out. The driver had
just whipped the horses to a trot when a rider with two
big guns flagged him down and warned us to hide our
valuables -- robbers and varmints were on the loose,
stalking the stagecoaches today. At hearing this, I
began to pat my face on both sides of my cheeks as I
sometimes do. Try as I might, I could not stop this, even
when commanded by Uncle. He then insisted the driver
take us back to wait for the train. He paid a goodly
price for our return. He explained to the driver that
the Cherokee Outlet was "too country" for his girls.
Uncle then chided me. He said, "You are twenty-one and
too old to behave like a frightened chicken. Cora is
eleven and she is not timid." I replied that my father
was dead and buried because of invading Nahollas who
had apparently killed him for twenty-five cents.

Uncle looked surprised that I knew of this heartbreak.
We rode in silence for a long while. He seemed lost in
thought. He then said that it was a great pity about my
father and that is why he and Aunt Emma support the Four
Mothers Society. He said that they are all trying to stop
illegals, the whites, from taking our lands -- and killing
every last one of us.

This was the first time Uncle had spoken to me in such a
manner and I was very grateful that he had taken me into
his confidence. I now observe that the eye tree is growing fresh branches, making me fearful again, and agitat-
ed. I will endeavor to prune the branches myself.

I prefer my pen to this typing machine that Uncle gave

me. But sometimes I cannot write fast enough to capture
my secret thoughts.

Si apela. Help me.

# THE ADA WEEKLY NEWS.

The State house in Des Moines, Iowa, is now on fire. No word yet on the cause of the blaze.

*Jan. 4, 1904*

Fire destroyed the Choctaw depot at Erick, which is a total loss. One arrest was made in conjunction with the burning. C.W. Jones, station agent, was rescued from the roof where he took refuge.

*Jan. 4, 1904*

**ADA BUSINESS COLLEGE IS NOW A CERTAINTY**

Advance his or herself for requirements of the business world. One would do better to enroll now.

*Jan. 10, 1904*

## THE PAWNEE INDIANS

The Carnegie Institution, which is carrying on research work in various parts of the world, has granted $2,500 to G.A. Dorsey of the Field Museum of Chicago for the year of 1904, for ethnographical investigation among the Pawnee Indians. This work will require some 3-4 years' time to complete and catalogue. It is proposed that he will study the religious ceremonies of the Pawnee with reference to the mythological origin of each ceremony. It is probable that the Pawnee in Oklahoma will be visited by Mr. Dorsey during the year.

*Jan. 10, 1904*

## CREEK INDIAN OBJECTS TO BURIAL ON HIS LAND

Muskogee: A peculiar instance, which shows the ignorance and prejudice which exists in the minds of the Fullblood Creek Indians, happened here recently. S. F. Romines, a well-to-do white farmer living on leased Indian land near Cane Creek, about 10 or 15 miles from here, died. The funeral was set and a plot of ground in one corner of the farm was selected for the grave, but when the Indian owner heard of the intention to bury the body of the tenant, he became angry and refused to allow the burial there. The ground was his he said, and no white man's bones should rest there while it remained in his name. All effort to find a plot on the adjoining land, which could be used for this purpose, failed, and the family was finally forced to purchase a lot in the Muskogee cemetery and the body was brought here for burial.

*Jan. 21, 1904*

**THE NEGRESS WHO SERVED AS POSTMISTRESS SUCCEEDED BY WHITE MAN**

Washington: The President has appointed W. B. Martin to succeed Mrs. Minnie Cox, the Negress, as Postmaster at Indianola, Mississippi. The Post Office was closed some time ago because the white inhabitants refused to accept their mail from her. Threats were made against her life and she was led to believe her life was in danger.

February 4, 1904

15 March 1904

After Aunt Fancy passed on, I began my experiments with
time, light, and the movements of the heavens in the sky.
I proceeded with the notion that words and numbers were
my allies. Once while still at Good Land I had asked the
small children in my care if they would help me with an
experiment.

Children, repeat after me, I said. In our language:

The table is on red.
Red is on the table
The table is on yellow.
Yellow is on the table.
The table is on black.
Black is on the table.

The letter is on the table.
The table is on the letter.

I then asked the children: Did you see the table move?

They replied yes and confirmed for me that I was on the
right path of study.

I am therefore writing my theory on the many lives of
time. I endeavor to explain it properly and have revised
it often. However these days Uncle complains that I
spend too much time alone in my room, therefore I now
write when he is out of the house. When I have completed
writing my paper I will submit my ideas to the U.S.
Patents Office. It is my intention to explain that time
is not the same for whites and Indians, and to patent our
knowledge before the likes of Mr. Dorsey from the Field
Museum come and steal it and claim it as theirs (as they
are stealing our lands). Perhaps one day I will return to
Doaksville to live and then I can be a teacher at Good
Land Indian Orphanage.

2 June 1904

Uncle has found me a job at the Ada Post Office. I was told that I need a strong back and an accurate throwing arm to handle first and second class mail. I wear the uniform of a postal clerk, a white blouse and a black skirt and a black belt. My hair is pulled up and fastened. Cora says I look severe and that I must remember to smile.

# THE ADA WEEKLY NEWS.

July 1, 1904

ICE COMES TO ADA IN HOT JULY

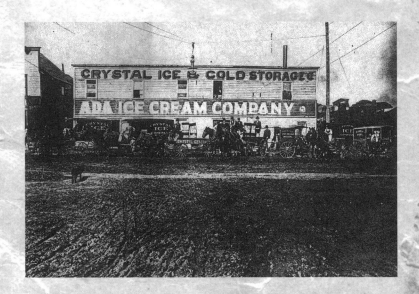

Uncle Henri and Lonnie Johns made the newspaper today. They are pictured standing on the fourth ice wagon from the right.

Ada, Indian Territory

4 November 1904

Tincture. fr: teinture. Yellow is teinture of jaundice.
The color of white gone bad. Mary O'Brien, my assigned
companion at Ada's post office, is yellow haired.

I grow weary of having a keeper and of being forever
reminded to speak when spoken to, and smile when smiled
upon. Mary O'Brien said I must look directly at the
patron who is speaking to me and that I must follow the
rules the President of the United States has set down
for all postal clerks. She reminded me of the predicament the Negro postmistress in Mississippi found herself
in, when white citizens would not receive mail from her
and the U.S. Government removed her, and that since I am
a redskin the same might happen to me. I did not tell
Mary O'Brien that the greatest numbers of postal patrons
in Ada are themselves redskins.

Si apela. Help me

Ada, Indian Territory
29 November 1904

Mary O'Brien said she had relations
with her cat. Well, I said, you have
something in common.
You both love fish.

Friday 8 December 1905

I made a discovery. Mary laughs at herself, the same as I
laugh at myself. We are a pair of giggleboxes when no
one else is around. She says that being maudlin is not
entertaining, and though she says she is not an enter-
tainer (despite how she looks), we must act maudlin for
the patrons. We are postal clerks, after all.

Mary O'Brien cares passionately, perhaps to a fault,
about what the citizens of Ada think about her. I should
add that she no longer has lice. She whispered to me that
she poured a small amount of kerosene on her hair and
then cut it very short to rid herself of the vermin. I
said I would be worried about catching myself on fire.
She replied, not if you had vermin in your hair.

Today at the post office she wore a scarf and a wool
bonnet to hide her tufts of hair and protect her head
against the cold.

Friday 22 December 1905

I have gained another valuable insight into my theory on the alternate lives of time, and how words affect time and space. We were accounting for the letters at the post office, when I suddenly said the following to Mary O'Brien:

The table is on red.
Red is on the table.
The table is on yellow.
Yellow is on the table.
The table is on black.
Black is on the table.

The letter is on the table.
The table is on the letter.
Did you see the table move?

Mary O'Brien replied that she did not see the table move. Then we both laughed, as is our custom while we sort and stack the mail.

That we can speak it, makes it possible to imagine; except for the likes of my poor friend, Mary.

# THE ADA WEEKLY NEWS.

THE NEWS HAS THE LARGEST CIRCULATION OF ANY PAPER IN THIS PART OF THE IND. TER.

VOLUME 6     ADA, INDIAN TERRITORY, APRIL 19, 1906.     NUMBER 1.

# AN EARTHQUAKE

## Early Wednesday Morning Wrecks the City of the Golden Gate.

## THE ENTIRE CITY DOOMED

Forty-one Blocks on Fire and City is Without Water---Thousands of People Killed and Other Thousands Panic-Stricken. Special Trains on the Way. Chicago Denver and Coast Cities Speeding in Relief Trains. Details Meagre as Only One Wire Reaches From the Stricken City.

### FATAL SHOOTING AMONG FULLBLOODS AT AHLOSO

*Our cousins made the newspaper in a fusillade of bullets. Uncle was thoroughly disgusted.*

Sunday 10 June 1906

Mary O'Brien and I each received a letter from the U.S. Postmaster. We are among the 28,000 women who work for the U.S. Post Offices throughout the country.

This past Thursday, Miko Kings hosted a three-game series with McAlester. Hope had once pitched for Hartshorne, a small town close to McAlester, so he knew most of the ball players.

Thanks to Uncle's *laissez faire* approach to business, gamblers like Mr. Beauregard Hash are buying shares of the team and Uncle's Indian Baseball League. Uncle has asked Mr. Hash to curb his appetite for liquor, floozies and gambling. I offer this as proof of what I mean.

The betting in this series started out reasonable enough, but McAlester won all three games and our team was out a wad of money. McAlester had a home game scheduled for Sunday afternoon, and Mr. Hash said he "weren't about to let them leave with all that money." Hash cut another big deal and if MK hadn't won, Uncle would have lost the team, the ballpark and the league. As it was, McAlester agreed to play one more quick game at eight o'clock this morning, for double or nothing. Cora and I feared that playing ball on Sunday and gambling on the games has scandalized the whole town.

But Hope drew on something from within him, the likes I have never seen before. He has always had an odd delivery of the ball, at least that is what Uncle says, but this time when Hope looked up into the sky he disappeared completely on the mound. For a split second the sky cracked open and a blinding light flashed on the ball field. McAlester's batter at home plate appeared to have been already struck out before Hope released the ball. Thanks to the branches of the eye tree I was not momentarily blinded as was everyone else was. Uncle and Cora said for me to hush as I was alarming people again with my bad deportment.

Hope struck out another batter in the same manner. Time had moved backward and then forward, I am certain of this. However it didn't help us later when, around 12 o'clock, a fight broke out. Uncle, Lonnie Johns, Mr. Hash, and all our boys on the team survived with a few black eyes. But we won the game 7–4.

Saturday 1 December 1906

Insulated. fr: isolé or Ezol or Izola. This is the elegance of chance. My twin sister and I were nearly a single event. Evangeline died and insulated me against death. Therefore I am called Ezol. Aunt Fancy named me for isolation.

I wonder if I marry and change my name, will I change my future?

Tuesday 25 December 1906

Christmas. Today was the saddest day yet as Great Aunt Emma died last Thursday and we buried her on Sunday. I was not expecting her departure to the other side, although Uncle said she had been ailing for quite some time. This was news to me and I said it. Cora replied that she believed her grandmother (Emma) died of a broken heart because we are losing the battle against allotment. Hordes of white people are moving into Indian Territory and stealing our lands. This is what killed her, Cora said.

Uncle gave Cora and me each an orange for Christmas. They are at great cost and most rare at this time of year. We will have them with our evening meal tonight and share them with people who come in to pass the evening with us.

Wednesday 5 June 1907

It is early in the season and this year, Hope says, he has mastered his odd delivery of the ball. The newspapers wasted much space trying to describe it. Finally they called it an "up-down," producing a ball that travels at lightning speed. Hope seemed pleased with that.

These days it seems that we are receiving new rules about baseball nearly every season. I am told that it is a rule that a batter who swings and is hit by a pitched ball is out. Aaron Johnson of the Kaw City Chiefs swung at Hope's spitball and the thing sailed and hit him on the point of the chin, breaking two of his teeth. Later Ollie Ellis of Kaw City tried to hit at a spitball that did break, and the ball punched him in the belly bounding out to Hope on the mound. There were two pitches and two outs in the seventeenth inning, and we finally won 11-8. Much later, after the game, Blip and I sat on the front porch with two glasses of cool water. He teased me and repeatedly called me "Big E."

"Big E." I like that. I long to speak in complicated thoughts to Blip. To write and speak well is a sign of a clear mind. That is what Mrs. LeFlore always said to me.

I have a nib and an elegant holder, blue ink, ink blotter, and stationery. Long before Uncle bought me the pen, he made me promise that there would be no more writing in the margins of books.

Lately I have had the strangest dream. I am old, and I am sitting beside my husband in the swing. It is Mr. Bleen and I am the Mrs. He is my clearest desire.

Thursday 5 July 1907

I'm partial to cemeteries, I said.

Light is the key to time, I said to Blip. Choctaw words
are tools for moving back and forth in time. Our verbs
are directional -- in or out, dull and bright. To "ball
up" is a verb.

A pitcher makes equations come to light when he throws
the ball. Ball + Direction = Light. And the light changes
time.

Blip just laughed and made a funny face. He said Big E, I
do not know about these ideas of yours. I'm just a Chick-
Choc.

I laughed.

Cora turns eighteen tomorrow. Perhaps now that she is
growing older she will begin paying attention to Uncle's
business concerns. She has only vague notions about the
ball game and its change-ups, but she has a terrible need
to become the object of constant pursuit by the
ballplayers, Blip included. Even Hope is not immune to
her charms, and he only has eyes for Miss Justina
Maurepas.

We have seen the pattern of a baseball field mapped
among the stars, Blip and me, and later I will draw them.

Friday 30 August 1907

Washday cobbler again. This coming week our chores will
be to pick beans and make enough lye soap to last us
through the coming winter. In two weeks the Twin
Territories Series will begin between Fort Sill's Seventh
Cavalry and our team. The first four games will be
played in Ada. Cora and I have saved enough sugar,
flour, beans, and ground cornmeal so that we can host the
men and their families for supper after each home game.
The final games will be played on Fort Sill's baseball
field. Unfortunately it doesn't look as if Cora and I will
be able to go to Fort Sill as Uncle has said we might
have to sleep outside in an army tent and that is "too
country" for his girls.

We have also paid extra for the town scavenger to come
and clean out our closet. We do not know how many people to expect for evening meals or how many guests will
sleep over during the first four games.

Saturday 31 August 1907

This evening as Cora and I were taking turns typing cer-
tificates of ownership for Uncle Henri, the infamous Boy
Howdy paid us a visit at our home. He is the green parrot with the cherry-colored head and arrived on the
shoulder of Mr. Beauregard Hash. Boy Howdy can talk.
Because of his charm, he and Mr. Hash are in demand as
dinner guests all over Ada. When Mr. Hash plays the harmonica, Boy Howdy says "Camptown ladies sing that song,
*Do-da. Do-da.*" I laughed and laughed as Cora did. She is
quite taken with man and bird. She confides that she
would like to marry Beauregard. I do not understand why.
He's handsome enough but splinters of ice shoot out of
his eyes. I explained to her that there are types of men
that are unsuitable as subjects of experiments. Cora
said, but he can play the harmonica and he has a talking
bird and he can dance. I said *Do-da*, and Cora hugged me.
I do not know why as she has never thrown her arms
around me before.

Sunday 1 September 1907

Cora was flushed with a youthful rosy color after she
attended the ice cream social out at Byng. After church
let out, Cora said she and "Bo" stayed out in the sun.
Tonight at home, as I watched her and Mr. Hash play with
Boy Howdy, I was seized by a giddy intuition that her
future is in grave jeopardy. I have never seen a man
kiss a bird until now.

Tuesday 3 September 1907

Tonight after Mr. Laemmle's photographer packed up his
Lumiére, we left Mr. Whimple's Chicken Farm and drove
the wagon to the DeSota Theatre. Mr. Laemmle made good
and paid for our tickets to see *Fickle Bridget*, billed in
the newspaper as a rip-roaring comedy about Bridget, an
Irish cook, Rudolph, a German grocer, and Mike, the iceman. Admission at the DeSota is ten cents, about the
same price as a ticket to a see a Miko Kings game. I sat
next to Blip and observed him and the others around me
laughing. I did as they did. What a relief it is to discover that I can learn to act like those around me.
Later Blip returned me to Uncle's house and we spoke
politely of the weather. Blip said his crop of baby red
potatoes are ready to dig. He promised to pull me the
"red thumbs." I love them with fresh creamed butter. A
bit of salt. They are the sweetest and unsurpassed as
far as I can tell. Then before Blip rose to leave and
return to Roff, he said *Chishno-ako chi-hullo-li*. I
replied, You are the one I love. Blip looked surprised as
if he thought I would not understand because I had been
so long in boarding school. I did not move a muscle when
he lightly brushed my cheek with his lips and said
Goodnight, Big E. At last, at last. Happiness.

Wednesday 4 September 1907

Cora, my fleshy, wide-hipped cousin and Beauregard
Hash are quite a couple these past few days.
She told me that they had not gone to the
ice cream social on Sunday afternoon but instead
driven her buggy out to the little prairie where
they sparked. What is sparked, I asked.

Foutre. fr: vulgaire. F-ck in English.
(I am not supposed to know such words.)

Friday 6 September 1907

Last night in the yard, flocks of ghosts prowled around
Hope's home on West Sixth Street again. Later we were
told by Marshal Bennett they were looking for someone
bad.

The Klan members carried a burning cross and shouted
"Coloreds s'posed to be living in Colored Town." I later
discovered they meant Hammond Heights, about five miles
north of us. Justina was terrified. She was shaking all
over. Hope ran out of the front door with a baseball bat
in his hand. Lucius and Blip grabbed their shotguns and
ran after him, and fired into the air. Our boys all disappeared into the darkness to chase down the men in
sheets who were molesting us. Cora and I stayed up with
Justina throughout the night and tried to comfort her as
Hope and Lucius and Blip didn't return until nearly dawn.
I read aloud from my constant companion, Evangeline: A
Tale of Acadie.

Fair was she and young; but, alas! before her extended,
Dreary and vast and silent, the desert of life, with its
    pathway
Marked by the graves of those who had sorrowed and
    suffered before her,

Passions long extinguished, and hopes long dead and
    abandoned,
As the emigrant's way o'er the Western desert is marked
    by
Camp-fires long consumed, and bones that bleach in the
    sunshine.

Something there was in her life incomplete, imperfect,
    unfinished;
As if a morning of June, with all its music and sunshine,
Suddenly paused in the sky, and, fading, slowly descended
Into the east again, from whence it late had arisen.

Sometimes she lingered in towns, till, urged by the fever
    within her,
Urged by a restless longing, the hunger and thirst of the
    spirit,

She would commence again her endless search and
   endeavor;

Sometimes in churchyards strayed, and gazed on the
   crosses and tombstones,
Sat by some nameless grave, and thought that perhaps in
   its bosom
He was already at rest, and she longed to slumber beside
   him.

Sometimes a rumor, a hearsay, an inarticulate whisper,
Came with its airy hand to point and beckon her forward.
Sometimes she spake with those who had seen her beloved
   and known him,
But it was long ago, in some far-off place or forgotten.

"Gabriel Lajeunesse!" they said; yes! we have seen him.
He was with Basil the blacksmith, and both have gone to
   the prairies;
Coureurs-des-Bois are they, and famous hunters and
   trappers."
"Gabriel Lajeunesse!" said others; "O yes! we have seen
   him.

He is a Voyageur in the lowlands of Louisiana."
Then would they say, "Dear child! why dream and wait for
   him longer?
Are there not other youths as fair as Gabriel? others
Who have hearts as tender and true, and spirits as loyal?

Here is Baptiste Leblanc, the notary's son, who has loved
   thee
Many a tedious year; come, give him thy hand and be
   happy!
Thou art too fair to be left to braid St. Catherine's
tresses."

Then would Evangeline answer, serenely but sadly, "I
   cannot!
Whither my heart has gone, there follows my hand, and not
   elsewhere.
For when the heart goes before, like a lamp, and illu
   mines the pathway,
Many things are made clear, that else lie hidden in
   darkness."

Mary O'Brien said she is afraid they will come after her family next because ghosts hate all Catholics whether they are Negro or Irish.

Si apela, help me.

Friday 13 September 1907

Blip asked me to define risk.

Risk, I said. There is the obvious one. Losing your life. Then there's the moral risk. Do you speak the truth? Do you stand up for what you believe is right? Can you die with that -- because that may be what it comes to if Miko Kings loses the series. Uncle will lose everything.

Blip changed the subject. He said we was all borned over at Alikchi some six miles northwest of Wright City. Big E, we are going to move back there on my granny's allotment once we win the series. Like all the other ballplayers I farm the land in the off-season. We'll keep the place at Roff and a place at Alikchi. That's what he said. It is not the proper English that I learned at Good Land and I don't care one iota about that.

Then later, after we put my horse in the barn, we heard a panther's scream. Her call, he said, is like a woman's moan. I looked directly into his eyes as I had practiced in the mirror. We sat down in the hay and he rolled on top of me and we sparked. And then once more.

I did not giggle.

Saturday, 14 September 1907

Iota. fr: tittle, not one whit.
Not one jot, Uncle! I care not what anyone
thinks of me. I will marry Blip Bleen.

Sunday 15 September 1907

There is comedy in spite of our grave concerns. In the
most intense struggle we have faced since Uncle mort-
gaged a portion of his allotment land to raise money to
build the Miko Kings' baseball park, he informed Cora
and me at breakfast this morning, in a most serious
voice, that we are dead broke. He said he'd spent all our
money and that if our boys lose the series to the g.d.
Seventh Cavalry then we are going to have to sojourn
back to the g.d. farm and eat g.d. red dirt. With that
news I quickly went to my room and fetched twenty-seven
dollars, all the money I have saved from the last three
years at the post office. I put the silver dollars on the
breakfast table. In the meantime Cora took out eleven
dollars from a canning jar. It was her egg and butter
money. Together we presented Uncle with thirty-eight
dollars. He was very nearly moved to tears. Before he
could speak, I giggled and, as usual, could not stop
myself. My bad deportment, as Mrs. LeFlore repeatedly
warned of, has ruined many an intimate occasion. But
this time Uncle laughed loudly as did Cora. We all finished a most pleasurable breakfast of fried ham, red-eye
gravy, and banana, before going off to church.

Monday 16 September 1907

Game one of the Twin Territories Series was today.
Blip's ball went screaming over second baseman Sgt. Ned
Hickcock's head, rising not more than ten feet off the
ground. Fort Sill's right fielder took one step and then
suddenly realized his mistake. He turned and started
running as fast as he could. He jumped, but the ball
sailed over his glove ever so slightly and bounced up
against a spectator, an Indian boy about 10 years of age.
Blip ran across home plate like a racehorse. We won 2-0.

Tuesday 17 September 1907

Bad news. We lost game two, 5-3. The men were feeling low after the game, especially Nolan Berryhill, who took all the blame on himself. They didn't come to supper this evening. It was just as well as I had taken a short horseback ride out to Uncle's "little prairie," as he calls it. I am fond of the scenery and the dense forest surrounding the prairie. There is a small stream nearby, and in some ways the land reminds me of Doaksville. As I dismounted and tied up my horse, I saw a legal notice posted on a tree next to where the squatter's shack had been. I immediately rode back to town to inform Uncle of what I had seen. However, when I entered the Miko Kings office, Uncle was embroiled in an argument with Mr. Hash. Regretfully Mr. Hash had wanted to purchase more shares of the team and the league. When Uncle refused him, Mr. Hash accused Uncle of being prejudiced against him because his mother was a colored lady. Mr. Hash said that to his way of thinking everyone on the team was an intolerant bigot, except perhaps Hope.

Uncle denied the charge. He reminded Mr. Hash that he had been allowed to escort Cora, his only daughter, all around town and that ought to prove that he was not against him. Uncle said the reason he would not sell him more shares of the team was because of Hash's relationship with Tom Bobbitt and other unsavory persons. But Mr. Hash would have none of it. He promised Uncle that there was going to be hell to pay and stormed out.

That was when I blurted out that hell was already at the doorstep as there was a posted sign on a tree at the little prairie that a woman named Karla Yurovsky was the rightful owner of the land and all others were trespassing. Uncle turned to stare at me. He told me to please go over the numbers in his "Book of Shares" and figure out just where we stand. Thanks to the eye tree, I was able to spot his mistakes in addition and subtraction in quick order.

Later, Albert Goingsnake came by the house and I relayed
all that had happened. Albert said for me to stop fret-
ting and pacing the floors, that the Miko Kings were
going to win the series and that Uncle and cousin Lonnie
Johns could handle a no-account scalawag like
Beauregard Hash.

Wednesday 18 September 1907

When it rains it pours. Early this morning Uncle visited the courthouse and was told that, indeed, the wife of the squatter buried on the little prairie was suing us. She claimed that Uncle had promised her the land, and the proof of this verbal agreement was the fact that Uncle and Leon Bonaparte had buried her husband "on said prairie." I do not know how Uncle can prove his side of the story since Mr. Leon Bonaparte passed away last year from a bout of typhoid fever. Perhaps his cousin Napoleon Bonaparte, our third baseman, can vouch for us in front of the judge.

This afternoon's game between our boys and the Seventh Cavalry will again be packed. Admission for the championship series has been 20 cents per game. Yesterday, the bleachers were full and we took in one hundred and eighty-nine dollars. A record. The seats behind home plate have been filled with the prominent citizens of the Chickasaw Nation. Ada's lawyers, judges, and ne'er-do-wells have taken the seats on the first and third base sides. Way out beyond centerfield is where the Indians with the largest families spread their blankets. It's far enough out that flying balls will not kill them and yet they can still watch the game. Uncle does not charge them. This caused one of our most ardent detractors, the old hen Mrs. Atkins, to claim that we favor Indians over whites.

Uncle responded by quoting Matthew 5:3-10, with the emphasis on the final passage: "Blessed are they which are persecuted for righteousness' sake, for theirs is the kingdom of heaven." Then he asked cousin Lonnie Johns to post a third sign at the entry of the ballpark.

It reads: "Smallpox, measles, mumps, scarlet fever, infantile paralysis, and whooping cough must be strictly quarantined until all danger of spreading the disease has passed. Persons with these inflictions must situate themselves way out yonder."

Saturday 21 September 1907

The headline in the evening newspaper reads: "Five Thousand Jammed Ada's Ball Park for the Fourth Game in the Series." All the merchants remained open until past ten p.m. Next week, the series moves to Fort Sill, and I am praying that I can go along with Uncle and the team. Cora has said she does not want to go.

Monday 23 September 1907

Washday cobbler, again. This time we opened a jar of
Cora's canned peaches. Tonight we are told that Nellie
Bennett, the marshal's cousin, will join us for supper.
This has caused Cora to speculate that her father has
taken a liking to Miss Bennett, despite the woman's igno-
rance of all things Indian and baseball.

I have no opinion on Miss Bennett, as we have barely been
introduced. However, since Uncle needs the marshal's
help with the writ against him, I think this may be the
reason for his sudden interest in Miss Bennett.

Cora said again that she wanted to marry Mr. Hash and
run off with him. I asked if she would call herself Mrs.
Boy Howdy. I said that Mr. Hash could not to be trusted
to tell the truth. Cora did not like that. She then said,
"At least Mr. Hash does not have an ugly scar on his face
like Blip." This caused a row, as I would not hear of any
criticisms against Blip. I said in a loud voice that Blip
was handsome and that a Ponca woman had cut his face on
the day she left him. I then explained that Blip's former
wife did not have any patience with baseball players, and
for Cora to be quiet.

We did not speak for the rest of the afternoon. I still
believe Mr. Hash to be a scoundrel, but I will say something nice about his cousin Justina. She is very kind to
me, and thoughtful. Justina corrects my pitiable French,
and she listens as I talk of my experiments with time.
She pays no attention to my bad deportment. She hinted
that she had an announcement to make after the final
game in the series. When I guessed correctly, she smiled
and said not to tell -- that it was her secret -- and I
promised not to reveal it. (I understand how to keep
secrets.) Justina said her surprise is her gift to Hope
when the Miko Kings win the Twin Territories Series. I
can see why Hope loves her so -- she is very insightful
and a loving friend. She whispered to me that she knows
Mr. Bleen has strong feelings for me. I giggled, but was
quickly able to stop myself, as any normal person might
do.

Wednesday 25 September 1907

It has been decided that I may go to Fort Sill next week.
Mary O'Brien will allow me to leave my duties at the post
office for a week, so that I may attend the final games of
the series. Uncle promised that if I get myself as far as
Richard's Spur, he will convey me by horse and buggy
(breaking his promise to forgo interacting with horses)
to the last two games. With modern travel as it is, I
should arrive by noon on Friday, October 4. There is
much to do in the meantime. We will first help Uncle
pack as he leaves tomorrow morning. Then I must pick
the last of the beans and can them before I leave. I will
hoe the remaining garden plot and pull out all the weeds,
then wash and iron my yellow dress and one other change
of clothing in case of inclement weather. I can take the
train to Pauls Valley. From there, I will ride another
train to Chickasha and spend the night at a rooming
house until catching the train to Richard's Spur, a
switch stop since 1901, located twelve miles north of
Fort Sill.

Much that has happened over the last few days is of
grave concern to me, and I have not spoken a word of this
to anyone. First, Cora came home tipsy last night,
around midnight, and began arguing with me about her
habits. I believe she must have been at a saloon drinking Choc Beer with that villain Bo Hash. Thank goodness
Uncle sleeps like the dead at the very back of the house,
or we would have had the devil to pay. Cora said in a
slurry voice, I'm not going to listen to you about
Beauregard. No matter what I've done, she said, he will
marry me.

I put her to bed at once. Uncle will be very upset if he
finds out -- and he will. I can hear him now, cursing
about the ruined reputation of his family. First the
Harkins, his cousins, kill a man, now this.

Only yesterday cousin Lonnie Johns said he don't care if
Hash is part Houma and part donkey, deep down the man is
a rough character and all his associates are bad too.
Tom Bobbitt and his gang of gamblers are going to end up
owning the Miko Kings if we are not careful.

Cora has now taken to lying too. When she awoke this
morning she claimed that she had been at the circus with
Beauregard Hash and not a saloon. I do not believe her.
Lucius and I were at the circus and Cora and Bo were
nowhere to be found. Lucius and I had been visiting all
the animals. After we saw the lion and the bear we went
to see Yulhkan Chitto, Big Mole, who was chained to a
cottonwood by his back leg. However, he had much room
to maneuver. Lucius said Big Mole spoke Choctaw. The
elephant lumbered toward us and cocked his trunk in an
S, snuffling up water from a trough and then he sprayed
me. According to Lucius, Big Mole said, "Halito chi
kanas." I did not hear this as I was giggling and very
wet. But Lucius heard him and was quite earnest about
this. Then Big Mole said he was sick with worry about us
and that we were all going to die. Little Mole, the smaller elephant, was very nervous too and would not approach
us.

Later we went looking for Blip but could not find him, so
Lucius and Hope walked me home. Then Hope went to see
about Justina. She did not come to the last game.
Lucius tried to reassure me that Blip must have gone
over to the Harris Hotel, where he sometimes stays after
the games. I was still wide awake when Cora came home
in the wee hours.

Si apela. Help me.

Throughout the rest of the night I read and re-read the surviving pages of Ezol's journal. Friday, September 27, 1907, a handwritten page, is the last entry, but the bottom of the page had been torn away. I study the picture of her eye tree. What was she trying to illustrate? Some kind of sensory data? Did she see multiple images? Or could she have had an eye disease as a child? Normally cataracts would have blurred her vision not enhanced it, as the drawing suggests. The eyes almost look like seven angry fish. When I look up "cataract" in the dictionary I find it means floodgate (of heaven). A large waterfall or any strong flood or rush of water; a deluge. What a strange coincidence, considering Ezol's actions with the water glass a few months ago.

Then there's Mrs. Sara Anderson LeFlore's letter of 1897. She uses the term "genius symptoms" to describe Ezol. LeFlore also says that the girl reads everything she can get her hands on, including French, yet she doesn't leave Good Land until she's twenty-one years old.

I find the photograph of the Miko Kings and study it once more. It must have been taken on September 16, 1907. Henri Day and Beauregard Hash are two of the men in bowler hats, the third man is most likely an umpire. Lucius Mummy is the big man in the back row next to Albert Goingsnake, with a mitt tucked under his arm. Hope I recognize from the Hampton picture. He and Blip Bleen are side by side in the front row.

As I look at the photograph, I realize there's another story emerging. Blip is the player I have been the most interested in, even before I knew his name. Perhaps it was the scar on his face. It's clear from Ezol's journal that they were going to be married. Yet she sent me in search of John Lennon and Hope, not him. Why? I can't help feeling there is something else that has drawn me to him. I lean in close to peer at his eyes, then pull back and gaze at the frozen image, half expecting him to speak. Watching him. I cannot name what it is I feel. Watching him.

I put the picture down. I must be off my rocker. Through the French doors, night is at its ebb. Somewhere down the alley a dog barks, mostly out of loneliness. Fireflies, a holdover from the heat of the

Oklahoma summer, linger in the yard around the marigolds and azalea bushes. They can't possibly survive much longer.

A small neighborhood cat is curled up on my lawn chair. For the past week, I've been throwing it scraps. Now I must either take responsibility for it or let it starve. I pick up the small calico, a she, I hope. It purrs in my arms as I sit down and watch the stars.

So much has become clear. As a young girl, Ezol must have been afflicted somehow. Otherwise why did she stay at Good Land until she was twenty-one years old? In some entries she seems utterly nonsensical, then on other pages she imagines time and space in the language of philosophers and physicists. Somehow she came into her own at the orphanage. She even imagines she will return and teach school there.

I also think I understand why Henri Day was in such a hurry to build an Indian baseball league. He wanted Indians from the Five Civilized Tribes to begin investing in themselves. To hold something in common, even if it was just baseball. When poor Indians didn't have enough money to buy shares in the team, Henri must have been underwriting the cost for them. That would explain why he was always broke. Plus, he was a lousy businessman.

I scan the shield of stars growing dim and look for the Big Dipper. There are so many things I do not understand. Electricity. The direction of time and space. Ezol Day and her eye tree. I doubt if she knew what was going to happen during the final game between the Miko Kings and the Seventh Cavalry. But, crazy as it sounds, I know that on October 5, 1907, Hope Little Leader will throw the last game of the Twin Territories Series. Why he will do such a thing is beyond me. But what happens to the team, and to Ezol Day and all the others, is tied up in this one game.

It's 5:45 a.m. I'm punch-drunk, exhausted by the weight of the past.

"Are you ever coming back to help me finish our story?" I say softly, looking up into the heavens. I shiver, suddenly realizing what I've admitted. I am no longer just the writer. I scratch behind the ears of the cat and bring another unexpected guest into the house.

And here too comes another echo of baseball's childhood memory in *Anompa Sipokni,* Old Talking Places.

When Henri Day pays the Miko Kings' week-long bar bill and hotel charges of $24, the barkeep grabs his chest, falls on a table, and keels over dead. Lucius and Nolan stand over the body, not knowing what to do. Within minutes the hotel proprietor rushes in and attempts to revive the barkeep, but cannot. "He was subject to fits," he says.

"I thought it was the size of the goddamn bill," says Henri.

# 8
## Portals to Other Worlds
### Ada, Oklahoma, October 16, 1969

Curving along the fertile hills of memory, an aging warrior parades a horse the color of turquoise into Hope Little Leader's dreams. The horse is hot and lathered from the arduous journey, but the warrior is cool and composed as he dismounts beside Hope's hospital bed.

The warrior wears a brain-tanned deerskin breechcloth cut off above the knees and cinched around his waist, the regalia of a *toli* player. His burnt red torso is so taut and smooth it fairly sparkles. A four-inch-wide leather belt is fastened around the warrior's waist and he carries two *kapucha,* ball sticks. As he turns around, he wiggles his buttocks at Hope, showing off a long horsetail that's attached to the back of the belt. This strikes Hope as a bit haughty, but he withholds comment. Of late, all manner of spirits have visited him. Sometimes when he's asleep, sometimes when he's awake. This is good news as it means his time is very short. Hope watches as the *toli* player turns to face him. He doesn't want to offend him by mistaking his taunting gesture, so he just nods politely and waits for another signal.

But the warrior does not move.

Hope looks around at the dull white walls of his room. Nothing has changed, as far as he can tell. The small gray metal chest that holds his pants and shirt is still next to his bed. A black and white television has been rolled into his room. It's on. Although the horse has vanished, the warrior remains at his bedside.

"Once," says Hope, looking directly at the warrior, "I knew many stories about ancient Choctaw ball players. I could sing the names of all the exalted towns in our homelands where the games had been played. They say the greatest players were buried near the ballfields. Maybe you know the song? *Yachou, Yacho, Calouche, Chula...*"

Hope's voice breaks and he stops mid-song. The warrior doesn't seem to notice. He's a rugged character, like all *toli* players. He has the tattoo of a handprint on his chest that many tribal warriors in the southeast use. As a small boy, Hope had played stickball with his cousins, and several of the older boys had the open hand tattooed directly over their hearts. But that was long before he learned to drill a fastball and his glory days on the mound. And long before the calamity that cost him everything, even the most inconsequential details of his life. Today, his memory seems to have ridden back, along with the turquoise horse and rider. He skips over his tramp years and all the decades lost to riding the rails, in order to recount his life with her. His greatest love.

Where is she? he wonders.

Hope drifts back to the spring of 1907. Their house on West Sixth Street in Ada. Indian Territory. He's found a patch of strawberries in the open field behind the clothesline. Each berry is smaller than a thimble. He pulls his shirt off and fills it with the sweetest fruit. Justina opens the screen door and spies the shirt filled with strawberries. Her generous laugh greets him. He puts his shirt on the table and pulls her to him. He feels her soft skin. Together they grope toward the bedroom. The dozen or so tiny buttons on her dress frazzle his patience. He wants to rip it off, but instead carefully unfastens them, one by one, as he says words from his reading lessons. Betony. Bibelot. Betrothed. She smells of fragrant, creamy white flowers, the kind she's just placed atop the bureau. He lays her on the white sheets. Kisses her nipples. Suddenly she rolls on top of him, taking the lead. Her red-black straddling his red. Her face next to his. Their copper sweat and slick washing into open, hungry mouths.

He moans. A foreboding blows into the room and the whole of her vanishes, swallowed up by blackness. He's lost her. His teacher. Lover. The woman he's come to rely on. But now there's nothing more to see except the straight darkness. Hope weeps, still in dreadful love. Still. But weeping somehow always transforms his pain into the belief that maybe, just maybe, if he tries hard enough he can conjure her once more.

Hope concentrates and enters the story.

The house on West Sixth Street is full of words and momentous events. A landscape of dishes, armchairs, and nomadic pallets amassed under one roof, becoming a place where her and Bo's friends—mostly friends on the lam—camp for a night or two. From them he's learned about Justina's life in New Orleans. How she'd suffered. But he prefers to skip those parts. He wants to be at the beginning of *their* story—when she is eighteen and they meet for the first time at Hampton. As she writes the simple equation "1 + 1" on the blackboard, he blurts out, "Equals four." The entire class laughs.

"That is incorrect, Mr. Little Leader. Come up to the front of the class," she says.

He jumps up and stands beside her. He remembers that her blouse is white and her skirt is dark red. She has such determination. They look directly at one another.

"I am one," she says, "and you are one. Add us and what do you get?"

"Two," he says proudly.

She smiles. "You may sit down, Mr. Little Leader."

He savors these moments. She is pleasure clasped to memory like a fastball to glove. Like a man fastened to woman's breast. Just as he feels their private past come to life, a crowd fills his ears. Hope opens his eyes and surveys the room. His guest, the spirit warrior, has just turned up the volume on the television set. The noise startles him back into 1969.

"There's a fly ball out to left. Jones is waiting...waiting...and he makes the catch! Folks, the Mets are the World Champions! Jerry Koosman is being mobbed as players barrel out of the dugout. Look at this scene! It's sheer pandemonium!" shouts Curt Goudy from the television. "But what can you expect? The Mets have a 5-3 victory against Baltimore, in one of the greatest upsets in World Series' history. The Miracle Mets..."

Hope hears the news and smiles. "Son of a gun! The Mets did it."

The warrior signs, "*Hopaii Iskitini,* in the distance our people gather together."

Hope yawns and closes his eyes. He craves a nap, but the warrior is irritated and claps his hands loudly.

"*Hopaii Iskitini,* wake up! It is the bottom of the ninth. Your team has a one-run lead. It's up to you now. Call the power. Call it to you!"

Hope tries with all his strength to sit up. After all, the warrior has just addressed him by his proper Choctaw name. He struggles to rise on his elbows, but he falls back into the hospital bed.

His guest shakes his head in disgust and transforms himself. Instead of *toli* gear, the warrior now wears a Miko Kings' uniform and a peculiar-looking ball cap. Sticking out of the top of the cap is a three-inch orange dowel in the shape of an upside-down carrot. The dowel points skyward.

"Wait a second, wait just a second," says Hope. "That's my ball cap. I always put it on before I pitched. For good luck."

The warrior ignores him.

"Hey, you can't wear another man's hat!"

The warrior ignores him.

Hope rattles the side of the metal nightstand with his forearm. He simply must get this man's attention. "Take off my cap! Who do you think fashioned that dowel into *fichik luak?* The blazing star is my emblem."

The warrior puts the ball cap in his back pocket. He winds up and throws a lightning ball that blisters the imagination of the spectators at the game.

Hope takes a hard look at his visitor and realizes that he's just watched himself strike out the second batter in the last game of the Twin Territories Series.

## Fort Sill, Oklahoma Territory, October 5, 1907

"It all comes down to this one last game," shouts Major General Shelby Thornton through a bullhorn as the Miko Kings begin to move onto the field. "While our rivals may have gotten lucky, the U.S. Seventh Cavalrymen are gonna send the Indians back to the reservation today!"

Hope watches as several thousand Fort Sill fans applaud loudly and whistle for their team. As the Miko Kings settle into their positions, Henri Day takes the bullhorn. "I only have three words for the Major General Thornton: *Custer's Last Stand.*" Miko Kings fans roar with laughter. As far as the eye can see, spectators line the fences along each foul line to watch game nine. Henri pushes his bowler back on his head. "Whoever wins this game will walk away with the championship title, and maybe gain the attention of the Major Leagues," says Henri. "Luck? No sir, we didn't get lucky. This is the culmination of six hard-fought months of ball play, and today I'm happy to say that the Indians are gonna paddle the behinds of the Seventh Cavalry...*one more time.*"

Indians from around the Fort cheer boisterously as Henri hands the bullhorn back to Thornton. The two men shake hands and wave to the crowd.

Two days ago, Hope pitched his most dominating game of the year and the Miko Kings beat the Cavalry on their home field in a 2-0 victory. Yesterday, the Cavalrymen charged back and their spitball wonder, Private Jack Stout, gave a brilliant performance, leading his troops to a 5-2 win. But despite Fort Sill being picked by the *Daily Oklahoman* to win in six, the Twin Territories Series is as even as it gets. Four games each.

Now, in the final game, at the bottom of the ninth with two outs, Miko Kings lead 1-0. As Hope takes the mound, he's finally decided what to do. All day yesterday he sat on the sidelines and sulked as the team got beat. What's going to become of him now that his woman has left him? Some of her last words to him come stinging back.

"You're too free and easy with money. You can't keep giving it away like it's water. My dear, you're so gullible, you don't see what's right under your nose. Your people are being overrun and all you can think of is baseball. What are we going to live on, Hope?"

"If the team goes under, we'll farm because we'll be hungry," he said, matter-of-factly. She'd looked at him as if he were a complete stranger, and walked outside. She didn't speak to him the rest of the day.

Now that she's left him, he's resolute. His mind is made up. He'll take the money that Bo and the others have offered him. That'll be enough to build her a proper house and take care of them both until he can put in a crop of cotton and corn.

Hope looks up into the bleachers and spots Bo Hash, the lanky man in the black suit and bowler. He's easy to find because of the redheaded parrot on his shoulder. How does Boy Howdy survive? Hash is obviously nervous. He jumps down a seat, nearly knocking an old Indian off the bleacher. It's clear he's uncertain of what Hope's going to do. Good, let him wonder.

Bo was the one that brought the sorry news that Justina took the train south to New Orleans on September 25, the Miko Kings' last game in Ada.

"Justina's done went home. After the Klan showed up at your house she was scared out of her mind. Said if you had any gumption you'd take the money we're offering so the two of you can make a fresh start. Five thousand dollars will go a long way these days."

At that moment Hope hadn't known what to do or say. He'd just stood there in his unhappiness and scarcely moved. Hadn't he promised Justina that he and his fellow teammates would protect her from the Klan? Why hadn't she given him a chance to prove it? Damn her, why hadn't she believed in him—just because he said he'd never dreamed of wanting to kill anyone? Then he thinks about how he couldn't protect his sisters like his mother had asked him to do. Maybe Justina was right, maybe he was weak.

"Don't nobody care, neither," said Hash, nervously grabbing a bandanna out of his pocket. "You think Henri Day or Blip Bleen, or any of the other Indian players, want some nappy-haired gal hanging around the best damn baseball pitcher in the country? No sir, they don't. Everybody knows Indians look down on colored folks the same as they look down on whites. Henri told me himself that I couldn't see Miss Cora no more and that I should move out to colored town and live amongst my own people. That oughta tell you right there how he feels about me—and Justina!" Hash covered his face with his bandanna and cried. "Ain't you gonna cry too?"

"No," Hope said. "I'm all the way past crying."

"Well, I won't neither, then," said Hash, sniffling and wiping his eyes.

Hope had never realized that Bo had such strong feelings for Cora. He turns to his teammates in the outfield. Maybe Bo was right. Maybe he doesn't know his own people. It never occurred to him to ask whether they approved of him and Justina being together. All he and his teammates ever talk about is baseball. Their averages. The best ballfields to play. Or the brutal ones that are as rough as gravel. Best double plays. Who's throwing the smoothest curveball. How to pitch to their rivals: Hartshorne, Krebs, or McAlester.

Hope takes a last look at his team. He would have stayed with the Miko Kings the rest of his ball-playing life. He steps onto the mound. The devil with all of them.


"Play ball!" shouts the ump. "Striker to the line!"

The first batter up is Sergeant Ned Hickcock, veteran of the 1890s Indian wars on the Northern Plains. Hickcock stands over home plate taking a few practice swings. His confidence is overflowing. Ned is in the prime of his life, thirty-three years old, and his batting this year is the best of his career. In the first eight games of the series, Hickcock's average has been over .500. But this time Hope decides not to give him a chance to show off for the crowd. He throws one strike, followed by four balls, and walks Hickcock.

Hope can tell his catcher is uneasy with Hickcock on first. He can almost read Albert's thoughts. "Not a single, not now." Albert flashes Hope the *fastball, outside* signal for the next batter. Seventh Cavalry's centerfielder, Private Benteen, is not a power hitter, but he's combative at the plate. When Hope's first pitch hits him squarely on the forearm, Benteen explodes and curses a blue streak. But he sees the field advantage and quickly takes his place on first.

At this crucial juncture, Hope now has runners on first and second. Blip, who's been studying Hope's movements, doesn't like what he sees. He walks down the foul line and looks into the bleachers just in time to see Bo Hash stand up. What's he doing? Hope can't be in cahoots with that no-account. But he's been acting a little crazy ever since Justina left. Bad timing, he thinks, spitting out tobacco. Hope's the kind that needs someone around to tell him what to do. Damn boarding schools. Some kids come out not able to think for themselves. But surely Hope's not mixed up with Hash and Bobbitt and the other gamblers? Blip signals to Henri and Lonnie Johns in the stands, then points to Hash. *Get him,* he signs. *Find out what he's doing with Hope.*

Hope sees Blip's signals and looks at him with pure hatred. Blip senses it and wonders if Hope knows what happened between him and Cora. He's disgusted with himself. He knows the fault was all his, there's no denying it. He should have never opened his door to that gal. But Cora was banging on every door of the Harris Hotel, teetering back and forth, heel to toe, as if on a ledge.

"Blip Bleen come out wherever you are!" she had shouted in a schooled, but woozy, voice.

"What's wrong?" He'd been half-asleep, pulling on his coveralls.

"Let me in. I need your help."

Blip doesn't know what came over him. She worked that spider magic of hers on him and he couldn't seem to push her away. Afterwards he found out what Cora had really wanted—for him to take money from Hash and his cohorts. In return he was supposed to make sure the Miko Kings would lose against the Cavalry. He'd rather kill than let that happen. What a low-down pair Cora and Hash are. They deserve one another.

But what's he going to tell Ezol? Hope must know. That's why he's seething—he's always been protective of Ezol. Like a little sister. Blip turns his attention back to the game.

Right fielder Private Philip Kearney steps up to the plate. Hope rears back and fires. The ball comes in just a little too high. It's clear from the look on Albert's face that he thinks Hope has wasted a pitch trying to get Kearney to swing out of the strike zone. But Charlie Wright, the home plate umpire, calls it a strike.

"Charlie, it was high!" shouts Kearney.

"You want my hankie? Dry your tears and get in there and hit," says Charlie.

Kearney is set to throttle the next ball, but the pitch is wild and outside. The count now is 1-1. Hope throws two more lousy pitches, both low and inside. Kearney doesn't swing on either ball. The count is 3-1.

Hope looks at Blip, then up into the stands. He sees Henri Day climbing over the fans with a baseball bat in his hand. Lonnie Johns is close behind. Hash plays his harmonica, seemingly unaware. When Hope had cut the deal, he had only one request: *Stop playing that goddamn thing during the game.* Hash can't even do that.

Hope adjusts his ball cap. Now the only question is what to throw to make it look interesting. Hope can see that Ezol has come down from the bleachers and is standing close to the dugout. Over the roar of the crowd, she's yelling at Blip, "One plus one equals four!"

Their eyes meet. *Stop, don't do it,* she signs. *Stop. Stop. Stop. Stop.* She keeps signing and screaming, trying to be heard over the roar of the crowd, yelling, "Throw the ball!"

Hope turns away. Big E, this one's for you. All these years you've been chanting that stupid equation. Now you get to see it in action.

Kearney's a lefty. Of his pitches, the most effective so far has been his spitball. He looks again at Albert, who's signaling for a spitball. Hope winds up and throws. It's outside. Ball four. Kearney walks and the bases are loaded.

## Ada, Oklahoma, October 16, 1969

"Seventh Cavalry won that game 4-1," signs the warrior. "You threw a big easy down the middle of the plate to Hugh Scott. With one pitch, one swing of the bat, you got four runs. One plus one equals four."

Hope crosses his wretched arms and rolls on his side. Remembering cankers his heart.

Just then, a white woman, the night nurse, walks into the room and turns off the television. She checks her patient's pulse. She notes his irregular breathing. She examines the morphine drip and makes a note on the clipboard attached to the foot of his bed. For an instant she considers the scrawny corpse-of-an-Indian lying in the hospital bed. Once, decades ago, he might have been handsome, when his features were full and round instead of deeply lined and elongated with age. She touches the old man's flimsy skin, translucent as dry parchment. She looks at his mutilated forearms and shakes her head. This was no accident, she's sure of it. Judging by the way the wounds healed, it looks like someone chopped off his hands at the wrist. How did he manage to stay alive all these years selling pencils, migrating from town to town? A beggar's salary would have paid more. No one visits him. His family must be dead. She sighs. Turning the old Indian on his left side reveals a bedsore growing on his buttocks. He doesn't have much time left anyway, she thinks.

Her patient groans. She straightens his catheter tube and wonders why the two night nurses work so hard to keep "No Hands" alive. Or why John brought a portable TV from home to put into the old man's room. He's nearly blind. The effects of diabetes. Weak as he is, she doubts he knows the World Series has just ended. She briefly ponders the pitiful old Indian's face as she pulls a thin blanket over him. Then she walks quietly out of the room.

When the nurse leaves, Hope picks a fight with the warrior. "What the hell do you want from me?"

"You know," signs the warrior, as he casually drops the ball. He then pulls an enormous headdress down hard over his braids.

Hope doesn't know, but he wishes the warrior would take the head-dress off. The feathers remind him of Blip's costume in *His Last Game*. Sweat beads rise across Hope's forehead. He's growing angry. Hope can still see Laemmle's face as he coaxed him off his horse all those years ago.

"The red man," said Laemmle, "will be celebrated like no other hero in moving pictures. Son, it will be your image that will be remembered as the heroic face of American baseball."

Even a bookkeeper from Germany understood Hope better than he understood himself. Laemmle sensed Hope's ambition was to become the greatest baseball player—ever. More famous than his uncle Ahojebo. More famous than Cy Young or Deacon Phillippe. That was all it took, a little coaxing from a stranger and he'd go against his best judgment. Then there was the game...Bo Hash was no stranger, but he sure wasn't a friend.

"Too much clarity," he says, raising his mutilated arms. It shouldn't be much longer, his thin flesh is dissolving like a shadow, and his hair long ago turned white, from thinking white thoughts.

The warrior snaps his fingers right under Hope's nose. "*Hopaii Iskitini.* Pay attention!" he signs, as he strikes a heroic pose. Depending on his stance, he appears by turns as a sleek and muscular young man, or a pitiful old man with an extended belly.

At first Hope doesn't understand the meaning of this shape shifting. Then it hits him. Baseball is a game without limits. Does he have the power, after all this time? At that moment, the turquoise horse reappears and the warrior jumps on his back. Hope watches as horse and rider bolt out of the room and fade into a streak of light at sunset.

"I want my hands back!" he shouts. And once again his memories smell of rage and her gardenias.

And here too comes another remnant of baseball's childhood memory in *Anompa Sipokni,* Old Talking Places.

Bo Hash plays a harmonica and keeps a vigil during
　the last game
*My friend, when you go away, you will sing like I sing?*
Boy Howdy chirps and strains against clipped wings
*My friend, when you go away, you will sing like I sing?*
Hash blows another dry C
*My friend, will you go away mocking me?*
One more time, bird
*My friend, this song is going away mocking me.*

# 9

## Reoccurring Interludes

### Ada, Oklahoma, October 2006

Around 6 p.m. I retrieve my neutered cat from the vet's office. A she. I decide to call her Calico. I spend the next couple of hours fussing after the stray I hope I can tame. I didn't have time for a pet in New York. Arabs don't like animals in the house, so while I lived in Jordan I followed custom. I haven't taken care of a pet in years—decades really—not since my father and I lived in Stroud and kept a little dog named Ginger. When she died we both cried and vowed never to have another pet. Now, I've taken in a stray cat, bought a carbon litter filter for her potty box, two bottles of Furminator deshedding shampoo and conditioner, a can of premium kitten formula (while she recovers from surgery), and four cans of minced tuna cuisine. What's next? A feline massage therapist?

While the cat was at the clinic, it occurred to me that I'd never tried using a blog to request information about the 1907 Miko Kings, *the greatest Indian baseball team in history.* I thought that kind of brag would get attention, especially in baseball circles. I give it a try.

Later that evening I walk out to the mailbox and find a large envelope from Algernon Pinchot, the professor I'd written to. He has answered my questions about Justina Maurepas, the woman Ezol had mentioned in one of her early visits with me.

September 25, 2006
Bonjour Mademoiselle Coulter:

I gather from your lively reportage about the upper Loire Valley in France that you indeed do speak French. I was very pleased to learn that you "Googled" the name of Justina Maurepas and found my articles on the legendary "Black Juice." Yes, I knew her well. In fact, shortly after her death in December 1969, I married her great-granddaughter Evangeline.

As you noted, I retired from Morehouse about seven years ago. Thirty years of "preparing young men to change the world" was enough. But Evangeline is still a decade away from retirement. She's currently the Dean of Students at Emory University, which keeps her much busier than we would like.

But I garden for the two of us. My latest passion. At present the *Miami Supreme,* a variety of gardenia with large white flowers, is about to take over the backyard. A small cutting I transplanted three years ago now encircles our patio. My goal after posting your letter is to whittle it back into a civilized bush. No pun intended.

Returning to the nature of your investigation: Yes, I had planned on writing a lengthy book about the Great Lady and her early life as an activist. Today, I suppose Justina Maurepas would be labeled a terrorist, or an enemy combatant of the state at the very least. At the time I met her, I was a fledgling assistant professor. My dissertation was about the rise of Black Nationalism in America and I was turning it into a book for tenure. My plan was to write a companion book on women in the movement. But despite spending the fall of 1969 interviewing her, the second book never materialized. I felt that because of my growing emotional involvement with Evangeline, it would be impossible to write an unbiased biography of Black Juice, as I had lost my objectivity. (And my heart.)

You are correct in your analysis of my articles. I did have to embroider much of her early years after she left Virginia. She did experience the Robert Charles riots in 1900, and in the 1920s she knew Marcus Garvey. But by the time I met Madame Maurepas, the only stories she wanted to tell were about her life among the Native Americans. Now, when I reread my notes on her, as your letter has prompted me to do, I realize the only words that still come to my mind concerning her life are "grief" and "isolation." By her own admission, she abandoned Hope Little Leader, as she had all the men in her life. The fact that her husband, Gerard Louis Maurepas, died while they were married was of little consequence to her. Shortly after they exchanged vows, she traveled back to Haiti to search for her ancestry. He died while she was away.

It is Hope Little Leader whom she claimed was her true love. Sadly, he was lost to her. But I believe she suffered greatly from what we would now call post-traumatic stress from her ordeal in prison in 1900. And think of what she experienced: most of her family had been killed fighting for the equality that would elude them. They were of mixed ancestry, and had foreign roots. Need I say more?

For the purposes of your investigation, the questions about Justina Maurepas that I am able to answer come down to this:

1) How long did she live among the Native Americans in Indian Territory? From what I can tell, only a year or so. She arrived in 1906 and remained until September 1907. A short time, but certainly she'd grown up with Indians in Louisiana. Her family was mixed. She also knew many other Native Americans from her years at Hampton Normal School for Blacks and Indians. Suffice it to say she knew Choctaws.

2) Are her descendents part Choctaw? Yes. But today they identify as African Americans.

3) Concerning her stories—can we understand why people like Justina might choose violence? Perhaps, although she herself deeply regretted many of her own actions. But that is how we often see ourselves in our later years, through reoccurring interludes of regret. *N'est-ce pas?*

The following are the facts of her life that I was able to uncover and piece together:

Her cousin, Beauregard Hash, spirited her out of New Orleans after she was released from jail in 1900. That much is widely known. What is little known is that Hash ensconced her in Thibodaux, Louisiana, for a time, where she taught school. Then in 1906, he brought her to Ada, your hometown. At that time, she told me, she reconnected with her greatest love, a man she called her "mercy," her Hope. They had a liaison that yielded a daughter, born in early 1908 in Houma. Justina called the child Evangeline (the grandmother of my wife). Her friend Ezol Day, the woman you mentioned in your email, suggested the name.

While in Houma, Madame Maurepas taught at a little schoolhouse for Indians until 1920. She moved to Atlanta that year, where she met Marcus Garvey. She became involved, for a time, with William Shakespeare, the chief of police of the United Negro Improvement Association, until he was convicted of murder. Her son, Victor Shakespeare, was born in 1923 and died the same year of whooping cough.

By the time I met Madame Maurepas, she inhabited another world. In 1969 she was ninety-one, and seemingly a pillar of New Orleans society. She lived in a lovely house on Magazine Street and was resting quietly when I disturbed her with my questions. There were moments when she sounded very bitter, but who could blame her? This was the end she'd come to. In some ways she'd come full circle. Her family had once known comfort. She returned to it.

Madame Maurepas *aka* Dusky Long-Gone Girl (the nickname Hope Little Leader gave her when they were in school at Hampton) *aka* Black Juice, the legend, these are all the same woman. She lived an extraordinary life, as did her associates. I hope this answers a few of your questions. Good luck with your research.

Regards,

Algernon Pinchot
Atlanta, Georgia

P.S. One more thing. During our conversations, Madame Maurepas told me that she had been devastated when she learned that Ezol Day had died in a fire shortly after she fled Ada. It seems her cousin, Mr. Hash, and Miss Day both died within days of one another. Evidently, a fire engulfed a building in Ada's downtown. When we study the statistics of how many towns and homes burned in the early twentieth century, we historians are faced with a death toll, largely from smoke inhalation, that staggers the imagination. Herein is a copy of a newspaper clipping about the fire and a torn page from Longfellow's *Evangeline* with a note penned in the margin by Miss Day. Madame Maurepas kept it with the rest of her important papers. My wife and I agree that you should have them.

I keep rereading the postscript of the letter. *She died in a fire*. All alone.

I try to make sense of what must have happened after the Miko Kings lost the last game to the Seventh Cavalry. Henri must have remained behind with the team in Fort Sill, and dispatched Ezol to go to Ada and save the book of shares from the gamblers who would disenfranchise them once they took over ownership of the team. Somehow, in trying to save the book, Ezol must have become trapped in the Miko Kings office. Who would have known about her vulnerabilities, her habit of becoming so lost in thought that she might not notice smoke—until it was too late? As for Hope, he would have to disappear right after the game, but where would he go?

I gingerly slide the papers out of the mailer Professor Pinchot has sent. Ezol had torn page 45 out of Longfellow's book and written a sweet, poetic note to Justina: *As you are the gleam of Hope's lamp against the darkness...*

I then read the newspaper clipping. I take a deep breath and try to push myself to really feel what this means.

# THE ADA WEEKLY NEWS.

## October 13, 1907

Fire claimed the life of Ada postal clerk Ezol Day as she was trapped inside the Miko Kings business office, the evening of October 11. The fire apparently started in the back alley in the evening hours, destroying two other buildings and several circus animals in their cages. Ezol Day was the only victim, as the adjacent buildings were empty. Her uncle, Mr. Henri Day, general manager of the Miko Kings, and his daughter Miss Cora MourningTree Day, survive the late Miss Day.

Cora Day was held for questioning concerning the burning, but later released. Several players for the Miko Kings are being rounded up for questioning, the marshal said. Funeral services were held on Sunday at the Presbyterian Church on Fifteenth and Townsend. Burial was at Jesse. Miss Ezol Day, age 28 and a spinster, moved to Ada in 1900. She was well known by locals and served admirably in the U.S. Postal Service, said Ada postmistress Mary O'Brien.

The article horrifies me. I recall Ezol's words: *The circus lion is burned up in his cage. A black bear named Bobby suffocates from the smoke. Blinding him first, the fire singes the rest of him. Only the peacocks survive.*

Yet the other details are even more painful. Learning the true identity of my grandmother. *Cora MourningTree Day*...she lied to me about her name, telling me that Indians in those days didn't have last names. Who was this woman I thought I knew? The woman Ezol called "Cora" was the woman who called herself MourningTree Bolin, my grandmother. All the years she talked about being "punished"...I thought it was for something abstract and benign, like not attending church. Was it possible that her "punishment" was for causing the death of her cousin? Clearly the marshal, and perhaps even the newspaper reporter, thought Cora Day might have been involved in the fire. I think back over all the times my grandmother lamented her faults. Was the sentence she was serving a long life of remembering? Often a clear memory is torture. Remembering the past can be its own special kind of suffering.

Ezol is my grandmother's cousin. I put my hands over my eyes to try to keep from imagining my dear friend *and ancestor* in those last horrible moments.

A body hugging a wooden floor for air.

Enveloped by smoke.

Assayed by fire.

I repeat again and again, *She died in a fire...she died in a fire...* At last I tumble down onto the floor and weep—and weep.

And dream.

"What's it like to be over there?" I ask.

"Haven't you ever dreamed of a love affair after it ended? Or a vacation after it was over?"

"Yes," I say sleepily.

She looks at me with passionate curiosity. Her eyebrows arch slightly. Nothing else in the room moves, not even the cat.

"Tukbrinin, yaa Habiibti. Bury me," he says. A term of endearment.

"Tukbrinin, yaa Sayyed."

"I see right through you," he says, mischievously. "You want to drive down the Kings Highway from Amman to the Dead Sea, where we can bob in the water like a couple of tops."

"We can go tomorrow," I say, pushing away the plate of falafel we share.

"Tukbrinin, yaa Habiibti. Bury me," he says.

"Tukbrinin yaa Habiibi."

## Aichna, Alas

I lie down, having already smothered in smoke but not knowing it. My body drifts downward in an almost comforting swoon, onto the floor, still clutching Uncle's book of shares. Lying there, I have what I think is a fine perspective on my life. I see the girl I must have been all those long summers ago at Good Land. Dark with dark flowing hair. Smooth brown skin. A certain vagueness in the eyes. Aunt Fancy cradles me in her arms as she rocks us both to sleep. *Ome, Ome,* I think she says.

So with my arms across my face, my eyes shut tight, I see the glowing red. The trunk of the eye tree is on fire, its limbs detach from my body and I am truly burning up. Sweat...no, perhaps bleeding from infinite wounds.

What will become of dear Blip? Uncle and Cora? Mary O'Brien?

Finally the spectacle, which I can only summon for a split second, is terrible. Yet hilarious. A vast heave and contortion, perhaps a laugh.

—My bad deportment.

Her mind slides across old news. A room of green wallpaper with tiny blue flowers where her daughter Kit was born. Cora drinks and hides it. She drinks to excess when she remembers his kiss, his smell. Sometimes doing it to herself with a baby, not his, suckling at her breast.

A shadow creeps lengthily behind her. Spies the baby girl asleep in her arms.

They spread the rug of silence between them.

The daughter should have been Ezol's, not hers. She admits it over and over again.

Then a papery kiss.

Cora cries and swallows her grief whole.

Years later, alone on her deathbed, Cora will remember the burning night of October 11, 1907. After Ezol's funeral, she crawled into her room and stayed there for a month. When she came out again, her breasts were swollen. She changed her clothes and changed her middle name to MourningTree. Later to Mrs. Hank Bolin.

Her father left her the house and the land and moved to St. Louis to live with Nellie Bennett. Forever after he disavowed her.

She shredded all the notebooks, all the frivolous stupid equations—save those in the mail pouch, which she hid in the wall of her house as if they were the bones of a baby.

Seeing now that the spiraling hour has arrived, Cora doubts which way to go. Whether in the direction of earthworms, or toward the light of oblivion.

# 10
## Take Me Out to the Ballpark
### Ada, Oklahoma, 1969

Even after all these years he still has nightmares.

They rode the two quarter-horse ponies into the ground, he and Bo Hash. For two days they cut a trail east across miles of Oklahoma Territory, then northward into Indian Territory. They only stopped to feed and water the horses—and Boy Howdy, who was tucked inside the rain slicker Bo wore. The two men rode hell-bent for leather until they got into Pottawatomie Country and saw the tree stump sign that read "Corner Saloon Open. Two Miles." Only then did they ease the reins.

When they arrived at Tom Bobbitt's place, they rubbed down the horses and hid them in a nearby barn. Bobbitt was as hospitable and friendly as he could be. He gave them a cabin to wash up in and told them to come to the bar for their splits. He also told his cook to prepare them a meal and brought in some jug whiskey to celebrate their winnings. Bobbitt explained that he would be taking over the Miko Kings and the Indian league, but only as a front man for a syndicate up north in Chicago.

"Henri Day and his idiot cousin Lonnie Johns couldn't have made a go of the Miko Kings anyway," he said.

Hope winced. "Bring me a jug of my own," he said. "I don't want to feel nothing."

"You're hungry, that's all," said Bobbitt. "That five thousand of yours will ease the pain."

"I'll have the same," said Bo. "A jug of my own, I mean." Bo fed Boy Howdy sunflower seeds and chunks of bread. "In a day or two," said Bo, "Hope and I will light out of here for Louisiana to find my cousin."

"You can't leave," said Bobbitt. "The syndicate's gonna want Hope to play for the team next season. Hope Little Leader is a great asset. He just had an off-day, that last game." He grinned at his two guests. "Drink up, you've earned it."

Minutes later, a stringy blond put two plates of steak and potatoes in front of them. She smiled and took her seat on Bobbitt's lap. She whispered in Bobbitt's ear and he replied to her in a language Hope didn't understand.

She laughed. "*Gatt faa,* Tom. In America, everyone for sale, no?"

Hope doesn't remember answering her. He thinks he finished most of the whiskey that night. Because he was unaccustomed to liquor, he woke up the next morning still blind drunk. All he could see was Blip Bleen standing over him with an ax in his hand. Albert and Lucius were there too. That much he is sure of.

Blip dragged him out of the bed without saying a word. Hope's head throbbed and he knows he asked for water. He looked at his hands for the last time. They were experts—marvelous in what they could do. Perfect.

The three men have Hope stretched out on the floor of the cabin. When Bo rouses himself, he tries to jump Blip with a knife, but Albert gut-shot him with a 12 gage. Blip makes quick work of it, whacking off Hope's pitching hand first, then his left hand.

Hope's eyes open wide and remain fixed on his fingers as they curl into lifeless fists. His whole body twitching now. The warm blood pours out of him. His mouth is open, but there are no sounds coming out. Silently Blip and Albert tie his wrists to keep him from bleeding to death, their purpose not to kill but to disable. Just then, Bobbitt breaks down the front door, rushes in, and shoots Lucius, then Albert. Then he shoots Blip in the head, as the greatest Indian hitter in history swings an ax into Bobbitt's belly. The sound is like a cleaver to a ham hock.

Bobbitt, muttering something about customers, falls to the floor. He never gets up again. The blond woman and the others bury Bobbitt, Albert, Blip, Lucius, and Hash in the graveyard behind the Corner Saloon.

What comes next, Hope's never been clear on. Somehow Karla Yurovsky saved his life. Who would have believed a foreigner, a Prussian—the very woman who'd sued Henri Day for his little prairie—would have known how to cauterize veins and sew up skin over bone? But she did, and for six months she even massaged his forearms to keep them from withering further. Often she smelled like an angel standing over him. Other times she smelled of whiskey and cigars and men as she wrapped and unwrapped the bandages on his arms. *"Gaa faa,"* said Karla, on the day he left her place on the river to begin his tramp days, the spring of 1908.


Now the time has finally come to finish it. The turquoise horse and warrior have returned to take him to the ballpark with all his skills and muster. His desire has never deserted him. He sees Kerwin pumping his chest. For some unexplainable reason John Lennon is checking his vital signs. Hope hears himself say, "Let me go."

He raises up the sea horses to make one last heroic catch.

# 11
## His Last Game
### October 5, 1907, Fort Sill Military Reservation

"Play ball!" shouts the ump. At the bottom of the ninth with two outs, the Miko Kings lead 1-0. Hope has Hickcock on first and Benteen on second.

Blip, who's been studying his pitcher's movements, doesn't like what he sees. He calls a time out and walks over to Hope. Theo, Napoleon, and Isom come in from the infield.

"The jig is up," says Blip forcefully.

By this time Albert is out on the mound. "What's wrong?" he says, spitting tobacco juice on the ground.

"Nothing now. I'm okay," says Hope. "I'm okay now. I can win this, I can. Let me finish the game."

"Are you sure?" asks Lucius. "Indian nations are depending on us."

"I'm certain," he says. "I'm part of this team, this family. And I can do this."

Lucius pats him on the back. "C'mon Hope, let's play ball."

Once again the players take their places on the field.

Right fielder Private Philip Kearney steps up to the plate. Hope rears back and fires. The ball comes in just a little too high. It's clear from the look on Albert's face that he thinks Hope has wasted a pitch trying to get Kearney to swing out of the strike zone. But Charlie Wright, the home plate umpire, calls it a strike.

"Charlie, it was high!" shouts Kearney.

"You want my hankie? Dry your tears and get in there and hit," says Charlie.

Kearney is set to throttle the next ball, but the pitch is wild and outside. The count now is 1-1. Hope throws two more lousy pitches, both in-downs but too low. Kearney doesn't swing on either ball. The count is 3-1.

Hope looks up into the sky to calm his nerves. Kearney's a lefty. Of Hope's pitches, the most effective so far has been his spitball. He looks at Albert, who's signaling for a spitball. Hope winds up and throws. It's outside. Ball four. Kearney walks and the bases are loaded.

Now Hugh Scott, the Cavalry's champion batter, walks up to the plate.

Goingsnake flashes a code to Hope Little Leader, who winds up and lets fly a doper.

"Strike one!" shouts Charlie Wright.

The crowd holds their breath.

Hope throws another lightning curveball, but outside.

"Strike two."

Hope winds up, looking straight up into the Sun as if in prayer to *Hashtali*, the Choctaw's source of power. He disappears inside it. When he pulls out of the light he throws everything he's got at the Cavalry. Hugh Scott swings again but just tips the ball, and it flies straight into Hope's glove.

And the roar of the Indians can be heard all the way back to Fort Sill, where, after twenty-two years, Geronimo, honored leader of the Apaches, is still a prisoner of war.

# 12

## The Center of the Farthest

*Ada, Oklahoma, October 2006*

Dawn is overtaking night. Light begins to reflect iridescence through the large picture window of my house. The enigma enters the room where we have recreated the past—telling the story of not just her relatives, but mine too. This time there is no hesitation. She recognizes everything.

This crisp fall morning Ezol wears a corn-colored linen dress and a scarf of the same color. She shoos the cat out of her wingback chair and sits down.

As we sit together for what I sense is the last time, I smile with all the love I feel for her. Savoring these final moments, I watch her carefully. Ezol's head tilts slightly back as if resting from a long journey. Her soft brown eyes influence her overall expression. They are neither open nor closed. Blind nor alluring. Rather, they are impenetrable. What they perceive remains subjective for, as she has told me many times, "reality is manifest from what we see and how we speak of it."

She picks up one of the ends of her scarf and fingers it absentmindedly. From where I sit, I can't make out the pattern of the blue-green threads.

"That's lovely," I say. "I don't think I've seen it before."

"This is the scarf that Justina and I took turns embroidering. I wore it to the very first game of the Twin Territories Series. What a day that was!"

"Yes, I know," I say enthusiastically, as I log on to a website.

"I've just been reading about the opening game on the new Miko Kings' weblog. There are dozens of new posts about their historic 1907 win over Fort Sill's Seventh Cavalrymen."

"So you have truly turned back time," she says.

"People have filled in a lot of the blanks about what happened to the team and the players. Last night I posted the photograph from the mail pouch...so you're right, Indian baseball is a game of collaboration."

Ezol seems amused. "It must be Nita Goingsnake's grandchildren. She was so proud of her father. Do they give the team's final line-up?"

"Yes. Shall I read it to you?"

"I would like that."

"Centerfield, Nolan Berryhill; Left Field, Blip Bleen; Second Base, Isom Joel; Right Field, Oscar Pickens; Catcher, Albert "Batteries" Goingsnake; Third Base, Napoleon Bonaparte; First Base, Lucius Mummy; Shortstop, Theo Porter; Pitcher, Hope Little Leader; and Batgirl, Nita Goingsnake."

"Just as it should be," she says.

"Listen to this: 'Hope Little Leader gets a signal from Blip Bleen on the sidelines and throws his famous "in-down" to Fort Sill's batter, Hugh Scott, who smacks it straight across the plate into Hope's glove. The Miko Kings win the 1907 Twin Territories championship in a 1-0 victory.'"

Ezol listens intently and smiles. "Blip will like that."

We look at each other and I suddenly want to jump up and run to her like a child who's awakened from a bad dream. But I don't, for fear she'll vanish and I'll be left alone again.

"Before you leave, will you tell me some things?"

"If I can."

"Why did I feel so abandoned?"

"Because when your mother died, you had no other real ancestors to turn to. Cora had a grief she couldn't bury, and you had no one else on your mother's side to take care of you. Lena, I may not be your blood grandmother—but I should have been. And I have always been with you in spirit. That is the true story I came to tell."

Her words wash over me like a warm blanket and tears roll down my face.

"Will you ever return?" I ask softly, grabbing a tissue.

"Yes, of course," she says. "As you know, I continually occupy myself with patterns and questions. The interpretation of time, the speed of love, the velocity of a meteor shower, or the time it takes for a small white ball to fly from the pitcher's hand across home plate. These things still interest me. As you have always interested me, my girl." She pauses then adds, "My dearest girl."

"As you will always interest me," I say.


Now it's my turn to become the movable object in space, a relative whose clock is set at my own distant future. Within an instant, the sheathing that has held us in place will expand, and although we are intimately linked by the motion of story, we are also distinct equations. I turn away and close my eyes knowing that I am a moving body in Choctaw space, as she is, and that miraculously we must both disappear…for a time.

Such is the mission of celestial knowledge.

Such is the sacred made manifest in the flesh of the page.

# Author's Note

*Miko Kings* is a work of fiction. While some of the characters are based on historical figures, it's important to remember they are fictional, like the story. However, there were many Indian baseball teams in both Indian Territory and Oklahoma Territory. The *Daily Oklahoman* sportswriter Charles Saulsberry mentions a team known as the Purcell Chickasaws that played on June 19, 1891, against the Pirates, a team from Oklahoma City. Saulsberry's newspaper series, entitled "50 Years in Baseball" began in the *Daily Oklahoman* on February 4, 1940, and ran for most of that year. Royce "Crash" Parr, baseball historian and author, was kind enough to share many of Saulsberry's articles with me. Parr's help and knowledge are greatly appreciated.

Some books were important to me in my research. *Cabin in the Blackjacks, A History of Ada, Oklahoma* by Roy S. McKeown (1980) is an insightful, self-published history that brought the early city of Ada to life for me. Angie Debo's *And Still the Waters Run: The Betrayal of the Five Civilized Tribes* (Princeton University Press, 1940) has information about the Four Mothers Society; much more research is needed concerning this early organization. *Reflections of Goodland*, vols. 1 and 2 (Northeast Texas Publishing Co., Mt. Vernon, 1993; Goodland Presbyterian Children's Home, Hugo, OK) was also helpful to me. Some liberties have been taken in terms of the spelling of Goodland. In the early years, the place name seems to have been derived from the Choctaw *Yakni Achukma*. Two words. Other Choctaw neighborhoods of the early Good Land Mission are also written as two words, such as *Bok Chito, Yashu Bok, Baiyi Hikia,* and *Lukchuk Homma.* Therefore I surmised that my fictional character Ezol Day, who grew up at Good Land Mission, should refer to the school in her journal as "Good Land."

Credit must be given to the newspaper archives of the *Ada Evening News* for allowing me to reprint the early pictures and articles from the 1904 editions of their newspaper. I especially want to thank Brenda Tollett, former editor of the *Ada Evening News,* who showed me many pictures of old Ada and had great knowledge of the newspaper archives.

*His Last Game* (I.M.P., 1909) is from the Library of Congress Motion

Picture, Broadcasting and Recorded Sound Division, AFI/Miller Collection. This curious fourteen-minute film is both a delight and an enigma (in terms of why Carl Laemmle's I.M.P. chose to label the fictional Indian baseball players as "Choctaws"). I like to think that it's because we Choctaws are great ballplayers—and were renowned as such—even in 1909. Others may not agree with me, but brag trumps in fiction every time.

*Ome.* (Choctaw for all right.)

LeAnne Howe is the author of three books, and a citizen of the Choctaw Nation of Oklahoma. In 2006-2007 she was the John and Renee Grisham Writer-in-Residence at the University of Mississippi at Oxford. She was the screenwriter for *Indian Country Diaries: Spiral of Fire,* a 90-minute PBS documentary released in November 2006. Howe's first novel, *Shell Shaker* (Aunt Lute Books, 2001), received an American Book Award in 2002.

Photo: Mikki McCoy

Her poetry collection *Evidence of Red* (Salt Publishing, UK; 2005) was awarded the 2006 Oklahoma Book Award. Currently, Howe is Associate Professor and Interim Director of American Indian Studies at the University of Illinois, Urbana-Champaign, and teaches in the M.F.A. program there. She divides her time between her home in Ada, Oklahoma, and her academic life in Illinois.

Aunt Lute Books is a multicultural women's press that has been committed to publishing high quality, culturally diverse literature since 1982. In 1990, the Aunt Lute Foundation was formed as a non-profit corporation to publish and distribute books that reflect the complex truths of women's lives and to present voices that are underrepresented in mainstream publishing. We seek work that explores the specificities of the very different histories from which we come, and the possibilities for personal and social change.

Please contact us if you would like a free catalog of our books or if you wish to be on our mailing list for news of future titles. You may buy books from our website, by phoning in a credit card order, or by mailing a check with the catalog order form.


Aunt Lute Books
P.O. Box 410687
San Francisco, CA 94141
415.826.1300
www.auntlute.com
books@auntlute.com


This book would not have been possible without the kind contributions of the Aunt Lute Founding Friends:


Anonymous Donor            Diana Harris

Anonymous Donor            Phoebe Robins Hunter

Rusty Barcelo              Diane Mosbacher, M.D., Ph.D.

Marian Bremer              Sara Paretsky

Marta Drury                William Preston, Jr.

Diane Goldstein            Elise Rymer Turner